F

The MOST IMPORTANT THING

By

JEAN URE

SUPERMOUSE
YOU TWO

The MOST IMPORTANT THING

JEAN URE

Illustrated by
ELLEN EAGLE

WILLIAM MORROW & COMPANY, INC.
New York

Text copyright © 1985 by Jean Ure
First published in Great Britain
in March 1985 under the title *NICOLA MIMOSA*
by Hutchinson Junior Books, Ltd.
An imprint of the Hutchinson Publishing Group
17–21 Conway Street, London W1P 6JD
Illustrations copyright © 1986 by Ellen Eagle
All rights reserved.
No part of this book may be reproduced
or utilized in any form or by any means, electronic or
mechanical, including photocopying, recording or by any
information storage and retrieval system, without
permission in writing from the Publisher.
Inquiries should be addressed to
William Morrow and Company, Inc.,
105 Madison Avenue,
New York, NY 10016.
Printed in the United States of America.
1   2   3   4   5   6   7   8   9   10

Library of Congress Cataloging-in-Publication Data
Ure, Jean.
The most important thing.
Summary: Once out of the shadow of her talented
and spoiled sister, fourteen-year-old Nicola begins to
seriously pursue ballet even though she has doubts
about making a long-term commitment. A sequel to
"Supermouse."
[1. Ballet dancing—Fiction. 2. Sisters—Fiction]
I. Eagle, Ellen. ill. II. Title.
PZ7.U64Mo   1986   [Fic]   85-25917
ISBN 0-688-05859-0

64574

The
MOST
IMPORTANT
THING

CHAPTER ✤ One

"Look here!" Cheryl Walsh stabbed a finger onto the page of biology notes she was copying. She sounded aggrieved. "What's this s'posed to be? *Anthem*?"

The question was greeted with silence, since both of her companions were preoccupied—one practicing ballet steps, using the back of a chair as a convenient handrail; the other cramming her mouth with pieces of chocolate.

"I thought anthems were what you got in church. I didn't know *flowers* had them." In red ink Cheryl drew a wobbly picture of something that might or might not have been a daffodil or possibly a tulip. *Anthem*, she wrote and then drew a big arrow. "Thought anthems were things you *sung*."

More silence.

"Well," said Cheryl, "aren't they?"

"How should I know?" Sarah Mason broke off another piece of chocolate and laid it lovingly on her tongue. "Ask her." She jerked her head toward Nicola, who was still busily practicing her ballet foot-work, *battements tendus*. "She's the expert."

Since Sarah was speaking with her mouth three-quarters full of chocolate, this came out as "Jeez theggzpirt." Nicola, however, seemed to understand it. She paused briefly in her *battements*.

"Who said?"

"Zrijjson."

"Miss Richardson? When?"

"Other day." Sarah stashed her chocolate into a back pocket, there to let it linger and melt all by itself. "When she was going on about me being lazy, and I said I was only lazy with things I didn't like and I didn't like biology, and she said, 'Well, that's up to you, but I won't have you distracting Nicola ... I have high hopes for Nicola Bruce.' That's what she said."

"Wonder what she meant?"

"Meant she had high hopes," said Cheryl. Cheryl was an expert at stating the obvious. "Thinks you'll go to college and study all about anthems."

"An*thers,*" said Nicola. "With an *r.*"

"Oh!" Cheryl peered more closely at her notebook. "So it is ... I knew anthems were what you got in church."

"I nearly told her," said Sarah. "I nearly said she's wasting her time 'cause you're going to study ballet."

Nicola looked anxious.

"I hope you didn't?"

"I said I *nearly* did."

"Why, anyway?" Cheryl, busy obliterating the word anthem beneath several layers of red ink, spoke

without bothering to look up. "Everyone knows you're going to study ballet."

"No, they don't ... *I* don't."

"Your mother does."

"She doesn't *know,*" said Nicola. "Nobody actually *knows.*"

"She goes on as if she does."

"Yes, well—" Sometimes Mrs. Bruce got a bit carried away. There was nothing she would like more than to have Nicola at ballet school. Then she would be able to boast, "My elder daughter, Nicola, who's training to be a dancer," just as now she boasted, "My younger daughter, Rose, who's training to be an actress."

"Don't you want to?" said Sarah.

Nicola paused, one foot arched in its proper school shoe, a solid black lace-up with a broad, flat heel. (Mrs. Bruce wouldn't let her wear shoes with wedge-shaped heels or sandals with straps slung over the heels or anything exciting.)

"Don't know whether I'm good enough."

"Course you are." That was Cheryl again, stating what seemed to her to be the obvious. "You're a lot better than Janice Martin."

Anyone could be a lot better than Janice Martin. Being a lot better than her didn't prove a thing, and even if it did—well, even if it did, she still wasn't *certain.* Not absolutely one-hundred percent. Not enough to have her friends go around telling people about it, especially people like Miss Richardson, who had high hopes. Nicola looked over Cheryl's shoulder at the mess in her biology notebook.

"You don't spell 'photosynthesis' like that."

"So how *do* you spell it?"

"With a *Ph* and a *y* in the middle. And it's not *an-thems,* it's *anthers.* D'you want to copy mine?" She picked up her book bag and rooted through the contents: gym shoes, T-shirt, *Math II, Africa Today,* an apple for morning break that she hadn't yet eaten. "Anyone want an apple?"

"No thanks," said Cheryl.

"No thanks," said Sarah.

Nicola made a face and put the apple back. Denny would eat it. He ate most of the things she didn't want—apples, yogurt, horrible crunchy snacks from the health food store. He wasn't fussy.

"Here you are." She dropped her biology notebook on top of Cheryl's and turned, without too much hope, to Sarah. "Give us a bit of chocolate?"

"No," said Sarah.

"Go on!"

"No."

"Just a teeny bit—"

"Your mom'll be mad," said Cheryl.

"My mom won't even know!"

"She will. She'll ask us." Sarah, self-righteous, wrapped up the last few squares of chocolate. She did it very carefully, tucking in the edges and making a neat little package. "She made us promise . . . don't let Nicola gorge herself."

"I don't want to gorge myself! All I want is one teeny piece."

"It'll show up," said Cheryl. "Chocolate's got millions of calories. Millions and millions."

Nicola sighed. There had once been a time several years ago when she had been eleven, when she hadn't had to bother about calories. Mrs. Bruce had even complained, then, that she was too thin and needed fattening up.

"Look at you," she used to grumble, as if it were Nicola's fault, "skinny as a rake."

Those had been the days of peanut butter sandwiches and strawberry milk shakes and as many helpings of french fries as she could manage, in the hope that it would make her pretty and plump like her younger sister Rose. It never had, and it was Nicola's belief that it never would since, after all, she was *still* skinny as a rake in spite of sometimes secretly glutting herself on bags of popcorn and salted nuts. Nicola was so extremely skinny that a group of new and impudent sixth-graders had even nicknamed her Spiderman, but now that she was going to be a ballet dancer and be as famous as Rose (whom everyone had always said was going to become famous) Mrs. Bruce wasn't taking any chances: Nicola was weighed once a week and measured every month. Not that anybody could do anything to stop her growing *up*ward—she was already taller than most of the girls in her class—but at least she could be stopped from growing *out*ward. It didn't matter so much if Rose grew outward because with Rose it was just puppy fat and added to her charm, and in any case Rose was going in for musicals and acting, not for ballet. As Mrs. Bruce said, if you were going to be a ballet dancer, then you had to be prepared to make sacrifices.

There were some things Nicola didn't mind sacrificing. She didn't mind sacrificing peanut butter, or sausages, or whipped cream, or even french fries, but she did find it hard to have to sit by each day and watch as Sarah stuffed herself with chocolate while she was stuck with nothing but an old apple.

"You're a real meanie," she said.

Sarah grinned. Like Rose, she was somewhat rounded and on the short side. Also like Rose, she was pretty. Rose was pretty just as kittens on chocolate boxes are pretty. She had big blue eyes and chestnut curls and dimply cheeks all pink and freckled. People said that Rose was adorable. No one would ever have said that Nicola was adorable—*or* that she was pretty. Usually, on account of her hair being dark and rather lank, and because she didn't have Rose's pink-and-white complexion, they said that her skin was rather yellowish, which was apparently not a desirable complexion for a person to have. It didn't really bother her—not as much as it had when she was young, before Mrs. French had discovered that she could dance.

"I'll give you one little square," said Sarah. "Just *one.*"

Nicola hesitated.

"Well?" said Sarah. "Do you want it or not?"

She wavered.

"You'd better not," said Cheryl. "It'll put at least a pound on you."

"Oh! Horrors!" Sarah rocked melodramatically on the chair. "Fatness and hugeness and things that go bump in the night!"

"Janice Martin goes bump in the night."

"Janice Martin! Nicola couldn't *ever* get to look like Janice Martin."

"She might, if she kept on eating chocolates."

"She's not keeping *on* eating chocolates."

"She is. She had some off you only last week. You'll

make her get all pudgy and ugly so she'll be too big to dance. Then, instead of being able to say we were at school with Nicola Bruce, all we'll be able to say is we were at school with her stupid sister." Nicola's friends didn't think too much of Rose. "Rose Vi*tu*llo." Cheryl gave a simpering smile and stuck her fingers in her cheeks to make dimples. "Honestly! I ask you."

Sidetracked, Sarah said, "Are *you* going to call yourself Vitullo?"

"No," said Nicola. She said it very firmly. Vitullo had been Rose's idea. It had been the name of a teacher they had once had, and Rose had taken a fancy to it. She had said that Bruce sounded too much like a dog. Now, at stage school and whenever she did commercials or appeared in shows, she was Rosemarie (pronounced "Ma-*ree*") Vitullo.

"You mean you're going to stick to Bruce?"

"Why not?"

Sarah thought for a while.

"I s'pose Nicola Bruce sounds OK."

"Sounds better than Vitullo." Cheryl finished copying Nicola's biology notes and handed the notebook back. "Vitullo sounds Italian. She doesn't even *look* Italian. Why does she have to be such a stupid twit?"

"Oh, she's all right," said Nicola. When all was said and done, Rose *was* her sister. She couldn't be too disloyal to her.

"All I hope," said Cheryl, "is that *you* won't get like that when you go to ballet school."

"Don't yet know if I'm going to ballet school."

Nicola leaned with her back against the bench, tendrils of hair whipping into her face from the stiff March breeze that came flapping across from the park. The school yard was full of the usual morning-break bustle, dotted all over with little knots of pupils wearing the red sweaters and blazers of Streatham School. Rose had never gone to Streatham. She had moved straight from elementary school to stage school—the Ida Johnson Academy of Dance & Drama, which was in London, in South Kensington. This meant that Rose had to take the train up to Victoria Station every day and then had to go by subway, which she enjoyed because it made her feel important. If Nicola ever went to full-time ballet school, she supposed that she would also have to go up to London.

She frowned and shifted her position slightly. Over by the phys-ed building a group of boys was kicking a football around. One of them was black, but she couldn't make out from this distance whether it was Denny or someone else. It might have been Denny. She squinched her eyes, trying to see.

"You coming down to the Health Center Saturday morning?"

It wasn't Denny. It was a boy from ninth grade called Frank Woolgar. He looked a bit like Denny from a distance, because he had the same color skin and was the same height and build, but when she squinched her eyes, she could see that it was Frank because he wore his hair long and dreadlocked, whereas Denny's was cut short and curly.

"*Are* you?"

A finger jabbed her in the ribs. She jumped and looked around.

"Am I what?"

"Coming down to the Health Center Saturday morning?"

The Health Center was a place where people went to do workouts and improve their figures. It also had a room called the Treat Shop, where you could, if you wanted, just sit around at little tables among the displays of leotards and leg warmers and drink milk shakes to the sound of the Top Twenty. People quite often spent an hour or two there before setting off on a shopping expedition.

"I can't this Saturday. I've got a class."

"After class."

"I can't after class." After class she was meeting Denny and catching the bus to Selhurst Stadium to watch Crystal Palace playing West Ham at home. "I'm going to a soccer game."

"With your dad?"

Nicola made a grunting sound, which might have meant either yes or no according to which way you interpreted it. Up until last season she *had* gone to soccer games with her father; but then she had discovered that Denny also rooted for Palace, and somehow or other she had started going with him, so that now her father had to go on his own. It made her feel a bit mean, except that she and Denny liked to hold hands, which was something you couldn't very well do in front of a father. Not that Mr. Bruce would have objected—Mrs. Bruce might, since she didn't care for boys—but Mr. Bruce was a person who was very easily embarrassed. He would keep looking the other way and pretend not to notice, and that would embarrass her and Denny as well.

"Don't know what you see in soccer," said Sarah. (Nicola observed, with mixed feelings, that the chocolate had been put away and forgotten.) "I can't think of anything more *boring.*"

"Once on television," said Cheryl, "in the Game of the Week, someone's shorts fell down."

Sarah looked at her, hopefully.

"Did you see anything?"

"No, they moved the camera away."

"That's what I mean," said Sarah. "It's so *boring.* Don't *you* think it's boring?"

She turned accusingly to Nicola, who was now doing a balancing act on the back of the chair, stretched horizontally across it with her legs in the air.

"Wouldn't go if I did."

"It's much more fun up at the Health Center," said Cheryl. "Why can't you come up there before?"

"Before class?"

"Before the soccer game."

" 'Cause I don't finish till twelve-thirty. There wouldn't be time."

"Thought you finished at eleven?"

"Not anymore—it's been changed."

It had been Mrs. French's idea. If Nicola came from eleven till twelve-thirty, instead of from ten till eleven, she could work with some of the more advanced pupils. The later time wasn't really as convenient, but obviously you didn't turn down an invitation to move into a more advanced class and to have an extra thirty minutes. Nicola had three classes a week now, on Mondays, Fridays, and Saturdays, plus piano lessons every Wednesday with funny, little, dumpy Miss Caston, who had taught Rose. Tuesdays and Thursdays she had to spend catching up on her homework.

"Know what?" said Cheryl. "I'm really glad that I'm not good at anything. I mean, dancing or anything. I mean, it's like being an invalid almost. Like that girl who played the cello and wasn't allowed to play sports in case she hurt her hands, and Nicola not being able to eat properly in case she gets fat, and—"

"*I* eat properly." Nicola swung herself deftly back to the ground. "I eat properly. You eat junk."

"I like junk."

"Bad for you," said Nicola. Rose ate junk, and Rose had pimples, only you weren't allowed to say so. She anointed them every night with special stuff for pimples that was supposed to take them away. She got very touchy if you said anything about it.

From across the school yard came the sound of the bell summoning them back to the last classes of the day.

"Double crud!" Sarah groaned. "You'd think they did it on purpose."

"Could be worse," said Cheryl. "Could be a double period of math."

Nicola slung her book bag over her shoulder.

"Could be double *needle*work." Needlework was one of the few classes that she really hated. She didn't mind math, or French, or computer studies, and she positively enjoyed English and biology, but whenever they had needlework, she ended up quite hot and bothered and cross. Mrs. Hibbert had said to her once, "I'm surprised at you, Nicola! Surely you don't make all this fuss every time you have to darn a pair of pointe shoes?" She didn't, but only because it was a necessary evil and because Mrs. Bruce wouldn't do it for her. She hadn't done it for Rose, she said, and she didn't see why she should do it for Nicola. If Nicola was going to be a dancer, then she must learn how to darn her own pointe shoes.

As they jostled through the swinging doors into the main school building, Sarah suddenly leaned across Nicola and, pointedly addressing Cheryl, in a loud stage whisper, said, "Don't look now, but someone's coming. . . ."

Nicola turned her head and saw Denny among the crowd. Very solemnly he closed one eye. Equally solemnly Nicola closed one in return. It was their secret signal. The first wink meant *Are we walking home together after school?* The second wink signaled *Yes*.

Satisfied, Nicola peeled off toward the science wing for two periods of biology with Miss Richardson. Cheryl and Sarah went along with her.

"Ah, love!" cried Sarah. "What a wondrous thing!"

Cheryl swooned and staggered into the wall.

"My heart is like a watered shoot—"

"A singing bird, you idiot!" Nicola was too used to their taunts by now to be thrown into confusion. *"My heart is like a singing bird—"*

"Well, you said it," said Cheryl. She giggled. "Not me!"

CHAPTER ❧ Two

"Y'know Frank Woolgar?" said Denny.

"The one with the dreadlocks?"

"Yeah, the Rastafarian. You know what he said to me?"

"No."

"He said I shouldn't be going out with you."

"What did he say that for?" Nicola was indignant. What business was it of Frank Woolgar's whom Denny went out with? And why shouldn't he go out with her, anyway?

"Says I'm betraying the cause," said Denny.

"What *cause?*"

"Some cause he's into ... black consciousness or something. Says we all got to stick together."

Nicola looked at him rather anxiously.

"So what did you say?"

"What do you think I said?"

"Don't know."

Denny grinned and swung her hand.

"I told him to get stuffed."

Nicola relaxed. They wandered on across the park, taking the path they usually took, which cut a direct line between Nicola's side of the park and Denny's. "You know Miss Richardson?" said Nicola.

"The one who teaches biology?"

"Yep. Know what *she* said?"

"What?"

"She said she's got high hopes for me."

There was a pause.

"What's that mean?"

"Dunno." Nicola giggled, suddenly embarrassed by her own boasting. "Probably not anything."

"Probably means she wants you to take it at advanced levels."

"Cheryl says it means she wants me to go to college and study anthems and stemtus."

As a joke it was lost on Denny because Denny didn't take biology. Seriously he said, "Would you want to go to college?"

She wrinkled her nose, considering.

"Maybe." It all depended on whether or not she was good enough to get into ballet school. Mrs. French had never suggested it. "I s'pose I wouldn't mind."

"What would you study?"

"Biology," said Nicola.

"What, plants and things?"

"And animals. And people. Perhaps I'd study medicine and be a doctor." She had thought of being a doctor once, but it was something she had almost forgotten about.

"What sort of doctor? In a hospital?"

"Mmm ... maybe. Maybe I'd go out and be one in India or somewhere."

"Wonder if they have systems analysts in India?"

A systems analyst was what Denny was going to be. Computer studies was his best subject. On the whole Nicola was more interested in people than machinery. It was only because Denny liked computers that she made an effort to keep up.

"Perhaps we could both go out to India."

"Won't be for years yet," said Nicola. It took ages to become a doctor. She calculated on the fingers of the hand that Denny wasn't holding. By the time she finished studying (if that was what she decided to do), she would be twenty-three. It was so far ahead as to be almost in another century. If she went to ballet school and became a dancer, she would probably be famous by the time she was twenty-three. Maybe. "Want an apple?" she said.

"Yeah, OK. Want half a cheese sandwich?" Denny stopped, dumped his book bag on the ground, rummaged around in it a bit, and finally emerged triumphant with a small tinfoil-wrapped package. "Here."

Nicola hesitated.

"Go on!" Denny thrust it at her. "Cheese and pickle—it'll do you good."

She took it reluctantly.

"I shouldn't really, I'll be having a snack any minute."

"Yeah ... one glass of fruit juice and a cup of yogurt." Denny knew all about Mrs. Bruce's food regimen, and he didn't think much of it. He didn't think an awful lot of Nicola's dancing either. He was one of the few people who didn't think that being a famous ballet dancer was such a big deal. "You've got to eat it. I saved it for you specially."

"All right."

Nicola undid the foil and took out the half cheese sandwich as Denny munched on his apple. They walked for a while in silence.

"My mom," said Denny, "says you need fattening up."

That was because Denny's mom was very large and plump. Mrs. Bruce would have starved half to death before allowing herself to have hips the size of Mrs. Waters'. Mrs. Bruce had gone on a diet at the same time as she had made Nicola go on one and was now down to a girlish size twelve, which was what she had been before she had started having babies. Sometimes she put Nicola to shame by going into changing rooms in shops that were really meant for teenagers and trying on short skirts and frilly dresses, just to show that she could still get into them. Rose didn't mind; she thought it was a big joke. She kept telling Mrs. Bruce how her friends at stage school "thought you were my sister." They didn't really, of course, but it made Mrs. Bruce happy.

Oddly enough Mrs. Waters seemed every bit as happy as Mrs. Bruce, in spite of not being a size twelve or even a size fourteen, but probably about a size fifty, if sizes went that high. Every time Nicola visited there, she tried feeding her rich, tempting foods such as sausages and fried fish and french fries, which Nicola had to say no to (because however happy Mrs. Waters might be, there was no denying that she was hardly the right shape for *Swan Lake*).

"She thinks you're too thin," said Denny.

"Not for a dancer, I'm not."

"She says you'll fade right away if you're not careful."

"That's what she thinks. I'm as tough as old boots. Just try me!"

Doubling both fists, Nicola flew around to the front of him and began pummeling at his chest, feinting and sidestepping as she had seen boxers do. Denny, with a jeer, dropped his book bag.

"Go on, then, Muscles . . . hit me!"

After a long, rough-and-tumble battle, Nicola found herself spread-eagled on the ground with Denny sitting astride her, his hands clamped over her wrists.

"Tough as old boots? You couldn't even strangle a chicken."

"Wouldn't want to. That's *horrible.*"

"Someone's gotta do it," said Denny, "if you're gonna eat 'em."

"Shut up!" She kicked at him crossly. She didn't want to think about things like that. It gave her a bad feeling in the pit of her stomach. How could she go on enjoying roast chicken if she kept thinking about people strangling them? "Anyway, they're not strangled," she said.

"No, they're hung up by the legs and have their throats cut."

Just for a minute Nicola felt sick.

"Shut *up!*" she said.

She kicked at him again; good-naturedly, Denny moved away. Faintly, from far off across the park, came the sounds of a clock striking the half hour.

"Heavens!"

In sudden panic Nicola snatched up her book bag. Denny bent to retie a shoelace that had come undone in the scuffle.

"What's the big rush?"

"I've got a class at half past five!"

"So?"

"So I've got to get back and have something to eat." She fidgeted impatiently, trying to hurry him. "Come on!"

"All right, all right, I'm coming." Grumbling, Denny picked up his book bag. He had said before and would no doubt say again that if you asked him, Nicola had a great many more ballet classes than were good for her. (What he really meant was that she had a great many more ballet classes than were good for *him* because they interfered with other things he would have liked her to do, such as going down to the Health Center to play table tennis or going to the local park and kicking a soccer ball around.) "You oughta stop doing all this ballet," he said. "It's very bourgeois."

"Bourgeois!" She buffeted him with her book bag. "Bet you don't even know what the word means!"

"Bet I do!"

"I bet you don't!"

"Bet I *do!*"

"So what's it mean?"

"Means it's plain ordinary, what all other girls want to do."

"Like going into computers is plain ordinary and what all other *boys* want to do."

"Not all of them."

"Well, not all girls want to do ballet either. Cheryl

doesn't, for a start. She says it's like being an in-valid."

"Yeah," said Denny. "I think she's just about right."

Nicola widened her eyes accusingly.

"I'm *not* like an invalid!"

"Yes, you are.... *Oh, Denny,*" he mimicked her in a small, high voice not in the least like hers, *"watch what you're doing. You'll hurt me, you'll give me bruises.... Oh, dear, now look what you've done. I won't be able to dance!"*

"Well, you *can't* dance covered with bruises."

"No"—still he mimicked her, going on tiptoe and doing a little twirl— *"and I bruise so EASILY!"*

"Only when people are rough." She pushed at him. "Go away!"

"Go away, go away!" He flapped his hands in imitation. "Diddums nasty wough boy make nasty gweat bwuises on her?"

Nicola giggled in spite of herself.

"You are a beast," she said.

It was impossible trying to be cross with Denny. They might argue a lot, and quite often they disagreed, but they never became nasty or said things to hurt each other, as Rose and Nicola sometimes did.

It was twenty to five when she arrived home, and Rose was already there, glutting herself on banana-and-sugar sandwiches and telling Mrs. Bruce in great detail, between mouthfuls, all about a new singing teacher they had at Ida Johnson who was absolute heaven and was called Ricky and looked like a film star. They all had to call him Ricky because that was the way he said he functioned best, and he had singled

Rose out for special praise and said she had an "exceptionally nice little soprano," and Susie Siegenberg was jealous as could be because he hadn't said a thing to her, and she'd always imagined herself as a second Barbra Streisand, which just went to show.

Having told Mrs. Bruce all about it, Rose then proceeded to go through it yet again for Nicola's benefit, even though Nicola had actually heard most of it while she was still outside in the hall. (Rose had a peculiarly penetrating sort of voice that sliced through wooden doors and brick walls as if they were made of paper.)

". . . and his name's Ricky, and he said we were to call him Ricky because that was the way he functioned best, and —"

"I know," said Nicola, "I heard."

She might as well have saved her breath. Nothing could stop Rose once she was in full swing. Not even Mrs. Bruce interrupted. She gave Nicola her health food snack—which wasn't yogurt but bran crackers and honey, with a piece of sesame-seed cake to follow—and waited patiently until they came back again to Susie Siegenberg and her terrible raging jealousy.

"She's absolutely as jealous as a *cat*."

"Why a cat?" said Nicola, but nobody took any notice of her.

"It's silly to be jealous," said Mrs. Bruce. "Jealousy never got anybody anywhere, least of all in the theatrical profession. She's going to meet a whole lot of people with better voices than hers, so she'd just better make up her mind to it. And why were *you* so late, my girl?"

Nicola, taken by surprise, choked on her bran cracker. It was Rose who answered.

"She was over in the park with that boy."

"Which boy?" Mrs. Bruce sounded instantly suspicious. She didn't care for boys.

"That one she goes around with. The one who lives in that horrible housing project over on Wentworth Road."

Trust Rose to know that. Nicola slipped a square of bran cracker off her plate and slid a hand surreptitiously beneath the table.

"You're too young to have boyfriends," said Mrs. Bruce.

Under the table a mouth opened, and the bran cracker was gone.

"You can't afford the time. You've got your ballet lessons to think of, not to mention all your schoolwork—and just stop feeding that dog! His manners are bad enough."

"I'm not," said Nicola. Under the table Ben thumped his tail. He was a dog who never could keep secrets.

"You are. I saw you! If there's any more of it, he'll be locked away."

Nicola made a face. She had heard that threat before. Ben was always going to be "locked away," to teach either him or Nicola a lesson. Once, actually carrying out her threat, Mrs. Bruce had shut him in the garden shed, but Nicola had crept out there and sat with him, and after only a few minutes Mr. Bruce had appeared and accidentally on purpose left the door open and let him escape, because Mr. Bruce had what his wife called a "soft streak" and didn't like having to teach people lessons. It was always Mrs.

Bruce who handed out the punishments, like cutting off Nicola's allowance and ordering her to bed without any television. Not that Nicola minded about television, especially if one of Rose's commercials was on. *Especially* the one for Dreamy Liquid, the liquid cleanser that pours like cream, and Rose at her most nauseating, simpering, and pouting and being Mommy's little girl.

"Finish up your meal," said Mrs. Bruce. "You've already made yourself late enough, hanging around in the park. I've told you before. I don't like you going over there. Anything could happen."

"Not with Denny."

Rose, at this, gave a knowing cackle. Nicola looked at her haughtily.

"What's that s'posed to mean?"

"Not with Denny ... *I* saw you, rolling on the ground."

"Don't tell tales," said Mrs. Bruce, who then turned to Nicola. "What were you up to?"

"Wasn't up to anything. I fell over."

"Ha-ha," said Rose, "a likely tale."

There were times, even now, when she could cheerfully have *punched* Rose.

"In the future," said Mrs. Bruce, "you come straight home, do you understand?"

"Can't if I've got something to do at school, can I?"

"Don't be fresh! You know quite well what I mean. I don't want any loitering, especially over in that park. Do I make myself clear?"

"S'pose so."

"Well, do I or don't I?"

"*Yes.*" Nicola snatched irritably at a piece of the

loathsome sesame-seed cake. She wasn't giving up walking home with Denny just because her mother had a thing against boys. She wasn't going to stop going over to the park, either. If they tried walking down High Street holding hands, some busybody would be bound to see them and tell Mrs. Bruce. They would just have to find a new route, somewhere out of sight of people who looked out of the windows of buses and then came home and blabbed.

"If you wanted," said Rose, "you could bring him to my birthday party—if you don't think he'd feel out of place."

"Well, he would," said Mrs. Bruce. "Obviously. All your friends are theater people."

"I know," said Rose. "Isn't it *awful*?" Complacently she licked a finger and began dabbing around her plate with it. "I just can't seem to get along with ordinary people."

"Ordinary people lead different sorts of lives, that's why."

There was a silence. *Dab-dab-dab* went Rose with her wet finger, blotting up the crumbs. Under the table Ben laid his big shaggy-dog head lovingly on Nicola's knee.

"If *I'm* going to come to the party," said Nicola, "then I'll need someone like Denny to keep me company . . . I wouldn't want to be the only *ordinary* person there."

"You're not ordinary," said Rose. "At least, not as much as you used to be before you started ballet."

"Yes, and speaking of ballet—" Mrs. Bruce tapped a finger against her watch.

"All right, I'm going." Cunningly, as she pushed

---

back her chair, Nicola slipped a piece of sesame-seed cake into the ever-open mouth beneath the table. "I still don't see why theater people are any different from anyone else. They're only doing a job, same as everybody has to. They're only earning a *living.*"

"That's what you think," said Rose.

"That's what I *know.*"

"You don't know anything!" Rose's voice had become shrill, as it tended to in moments of stress. "Acting isn't a job. Acting's a *vocation.*"

"Crud," said Nicola.

"Crud yourself!"

"Crud with gunk on it!"

"Crud with—"

"Be quiet, the pair of you!" Mrs. Bruce banged on the table with the handle of a knife. "Rose, get on with your snack! Nicola, you go upstairs and get yourself ready—and *stop feeding that dog!*"

CHAPTER ✿ *Three*

There are two basic types of dancers—those who are loose-limbed and supple, and those who are shorter and stockier, good at all the quick, sharp movements known as *allegro.* Rose had always been one of the short, stocky ones, Nicola one of the loose-limbed and supple. (Gangling, some people called it.) Being supple (or gangling) had definite advantages when it came to the slower *adagio* work—Rose had never been any good at *adagio,* her *attitudes* and *arabesques* had no style at all, and her *ports de bras* were simply unspeakable—but it was not so helpful for *allegro.* Rose could flash about the stage like a tadpole in a jar, her footwork as precise and exquisite as the tiniest stitches of embroidery. Nicola just occasionally had difficulty with footwork, and although she could jump quite high and always landed beautifully, there wasn't very much that she could do while she was actually in the air. Rose, according to her own account, had once done an *entrechat douze.* Nicola was never absolutely certain that she believed this—she thought, on the whole, that she did not—but it was a fact that Rose could be neat and nimble, apparently without even having to try.

Mrs. French had always paid particular attention to Nicola's *allegro*. This Saturday she paid even more attention than usual, keeping Nicola back after the rest of the class had been dismissed.

"It's purely a matter of concentration. You *can* do it—you're quite capable of it. There's no physical reason why not. When you come on Monday, I want to see you make a really determined effort. Otherwise I shall begin to feel I've been wasting my time.... If there's one thing I cannot tolerate in a dancer, it's sloppy footwork."

Nicola worried about it all through lunch. After lunch she had to meet Denny and go with him to Selhurst Stadium to see Crystal Palace play West Ham. Really and truly she would have been happier staying at home and practicing her *allegro* (as best she could, in the backyard). But you couldn't let people down—not when you'd made an arrangement. Especially not when it was Denny. Fortunately, on the bus on the way there he was too busy telling her about a program he had watched on television the night before to notice that she was silent; and once they'd reached the stadium, the game was everything. It didn't matter that Nicola wasn't talking, because even if she had been, he wouldn't have heard.

All afternoon, from kickoff to the final whistle, Nicola worried about what Mrs. French had said—*I shall begin to feel I've been wasting my time.* Did that mean that if things didn't improve, she would ask Ni-

cola to leave? Make her go to ghastly Madam Paula, as
Rose had done? She wouldn't go to Madam Paula if
she were the last teacher left on earth! She wouldn't
touch Madam Paula with a broomstick. Madam Paula
was all right for tap dancing and musical comedy
routines, but she'd never gotten a single, solitary
pupil into anywhere like the Royal Ballet School or
Kendra Hall. So much for Cheryl and Sarah. "Everyone knows you're going to study ballet." She wouldn't
be doing it if Mrs. French went and threw her out.
Which she probably *was* going to. *If there's one thing
I cannot tolerate in a dancer, it's sloppy footwork.*
Was her footwork really as bad as all that?

She arched her instep, inside the gray-suede boots
that had been a Christmas present from one of her
grandmothers. They were good feet. Mrs. French had
said so. They were strong, with high arches and three
toes very nearly the same length. That only made it
all the worse that her *allegro* was so bad. *There's no
physical reason why not. It's purely a matter of concentration—*

Around her ears, quite suddenly, the ground exploded. Denny, at her side, was jumping up and
down, thumping her on the back and shouting.

"We are the greatest! We are the greatest!"

Crystal Palace had obviously won. Nicola did her
best to feel excited (normally she would have been
jumping up and down on the spot with Denny), but
nothing came. How could she be expected to care
about Crystal Palace beating West Ham when Mrs.
French was displeased with her *allegro?*

"Did'ja see that last goal? See the way he slipped it
in?" Denny demonstrated as they left the ground.

"That was a real sneaky one. Wasn't anyone could have stopped that one. They just wouldn't have *known* about it, the way he edged it in."

They always spent the journey home replaying the game. Now Denny replayed it by himself. He had to, since Nicola could hardly recall a single detail. She made enthusiastic noises (*"Mmm"* and *"Wasn't* it?"), but Denny was not deceived.

"What's the matter with you? You flipping out or something?" He stopped a few paces away from Nicola's front gate. "Anyone'd think you hadn't been there."

She hadn't, of course, in spirit. In spirit she'd been back in the studio with Mrs. French, perfecting her *allegro.*

"What's wrong?" said Denny.

She took a breath.

"I'm worried," she said, "about my *allegro.*"

Normally he would have mimicked her. *I'm worried,* he would have said, all high and squeaky, *about my allegro.* . . . But today he obviously sensed that it was no laughing matter.

"What's *allegro?*" he said.

"All the little fast steps, the little body twists." It wasn't any use saying *entrechat* or *pas de bourrée.* It wouldn't mean anything to Denny. She showed him as they stood there on the pavement. He watched her critically, head to one side, as if she were demonstrating how Crystal Palace's last goal had been scored.

"What's wrong with it?"

"This bit, *here.*"

She went through it again.

"Looks all right to me," said Denny. "Looks pretty good to me."

"*Does* it?" For a moment she was heartened.

"Looks like Peter Nicholas. That goal he scored that time. Do you remember? The way he moved?"

"Yes." Her spirits sank again. What, after all, did Denny know? When it came to ballet, he knew even less than she knew (for instance) about economics, and that was practically nothing.

"Don't worry about *allegro*," said Denny. He slid his arms around her waist. "There's other things in life lots more important."

"Not to me there isn't."

"Course there is."

"There isn't!" She refused to be comforted. Just because Denny rated ballet lower than a hole in the ground—

"There is," he said. He leaned toward her. "There's this, for instance."

"Den-*nee!*" Nicola broke away indignantly. "Stop it!"

"Why? Don't you like it?"

"Not here!"

"What's wrong with here?"

"In the *street?*" Anyone could see them; Rose probably already had. And anyway, she didn't feel like being kissed. It embarrassed her that he should even try. He never had before. Why now?

"You're just worried about your *allegro*," said Denny. He turned and ran off. As Nicola watched, he suddenly leaped into the air, sending his scarf snaking up before him. "Stupid old *allegro!*"

Nicola sighed. Denny just didn't understand.

All Sunday she spent practicing *allegro* in readiness for Monday evening. Whatever happened, she wasn't going to let Mrs. French feel that she had been wasting her time all these years.

Monday came, and the session was grueling, but on the whole she felt quite pleased with herself. She felt that her practicing had paid off. Mrs. French didn't make any comment at the time, but at the end she said, "All right, go and get changed. Then come down and see me. There's something I want to talk to you about."

Nicola's heart instantly plummeted. Was she going to be told, in spite of everything, that her *allegro* was still so unspeakably awful (like Rose's *ports de bras*) that there simply wasn't any point in her continuing to take classes? She honestly hadn't thought it was as awful as all that. She'd been trying real hard, and even if she *had* messed up on one perfectly simple *pas de bourrée* . . .

"By the way," Mrs. French called after her as she reached the door, "that was good just now, wasn't it? Didn't you feel the difference?" Nicola gaped. "A lot better! You see, it's purely a question of concentration. Off you go, now, while I make some coffee."

Elated, Nicola scuttled off to the tiny changing room, which once upon a time had been a Victorian pantry and still had rows of bells above the doorway saying BEDROOM 1, BEDROOM 2, BEDROOM 3. She wondered, as she peeled off her tights, what it was that Mrs. French wanted to talk to her about, if it was not about her *allegro*. The last time she had invited Nicola to stay behind and have coffee, it had been to tell her that she was expecting a baby "some time in June," but that Nicola wasn't to worry, since she still intended to go on teaching. Nicola had been relieved about that because, even though babies were nice, she wouldn't like the thought of Mrs. French giving up classes just to settle down and be a housewife and wash diapers all day. (Rose said that was what people always did when they'd had babies.) She would hate the prospect of having to go and take classes with someone else—*certainly* not with Madam Paula. Madam Paula was a hag who plastered herself with layers of makeup, wore jangly bracelets and dingle-dangle earrings, and dyed her hair an unnatural-looking black. Mrs. French was blond and slim and beautiful, or at least she had been until her stomach started to swell up. There was no denying that having babies did make one a rather odd shape, all big and bulbous and sort of sticking out in front like a ledge. You wouldn't think a tiny thing like a baby would take up so much room. She hoped Mrs. French wasn't going to say that she'd suddenly discovered she was expecting twins and would have to settle down and wash diapers after all—not now that Nicola's *allegro* really *was* so much better. She was sure it wouldn't continue to get better if she had to dance for anyone except Mrs. French.

Suddenly anxious, she pulled on her clothes and hurried upstairs to the big living room, with its floor-to-ceiling windows and old-fashioned fireplace. Mr. French was in the living room, sorting through a pile of glossy magazines. Mr. French was a photographer. He took photographs of people who had just gotten married or whose babies had just won beautiful-baby contests. He also took photographs of gorgeously thin models and well-known actors and actresses. Last year, before becoming friendly with Denny, Nicola had gone through a phase of thinking that she might be in love with Mr. French. This had been exciting but also rather embarrassing because it meant she kept blushing every time she saw him and couldn't bear to speak, so that on the whole, she was glad she had grown out of it and could now manage to be in the same room with him without betraying herself. It had been very inconvenient, always turning as red as a beet.

"Hello!" Mr. French looked up and smiled as Nicola came in. (This time last year she would have been beet-red from head to toe.) "You're looking worried. What's the problem?"

"Mrs. French wants to talk to me."

"Really? Well, I don't suppose it's anything terrible. It might even be something nice!"

Yes, like *I've suddenly discovered I'm going to have twins.* That probably would be something nice for Mrs. French. She would probably be quite excited about that. Perhaps Rose had a point when she said that she was never going to get married, and that even if she did, she was never going to get pregnant. Getting pregnant ruined things. Mrs. French didn't look anywhere near as beautiful as she had before—and it was all Mr. French's fault.

Nicola glared at him, feeling for a moment quite cross. In return he wagged an eyebrow and made a funny face.

"I'll photograph you one day, if you're a good girl

and don't frown at me. You've got a good face for photographing—lots of interesting angles. Did you know that?"

She shook her head, suddenly shy again. She had always thought Rose was the one with the good face.

"Give it a year or two, you might even become a model. Have your picture on the front of magazines. Like this—" He held up a magazine for her to see. On the front was a girl with long hair and not many clothes. Nicola regarded it doubtfully. She didn't think she would like to be a model if it meant being photographed three-quarters naked. "Or this one—" Mr. French held up another. The girl on this one was fully clothed, but even so, Nicola remained doubtful. It seemed rather a silly thing to do, just standing around being photographed.

"What are you up to?" The door was pushed open, and Mrs. French came in carrying a tray and three coffee mugs. "I hope you're not trying to talk Nicola into becoming a model?"

"Why not? She'd make a very good one. She's exactly the right build, got exactly the right type of bone structure."

"That may be, but I happen to have other plans for her."

Oh? Nicola spun around, wonderingly. This was the first she'd heard of Mrs. French having any plans.

"How would you like to try for a place at Kendra Hall?"

"*Me?*"

"Yes, you!" Mrs. French laughed as she set down her tray. "Who else would I be talking about?"

"But—"

"But what?"

"Would I be good enough?" Kendra Hall was where Mrs. French had gone. You had to be really something to get in there.

"If I didn't think you were good enough," said Mrs. French, "I wouldn't be suggesting it, would I? Mind you, there's a lot of people applying and only a very few places, so don't get your hopes up too high. I happen to think you stand an excellent chance, but being good enough from a dancing point of view is only the start of the battle. There are all sorts of other factors to be taken into account. Height, weight, general health. They'll want to check your feet, check your back, make sure you're not going to grow too tall, make sure you'll be strong enough—"

"Far simpler," said Mr. French, "to be a model."

"Nicola doesn't want to be a model!"

"How do you know? Ever asked her?"

"I don't have to ask her. She's too good a dancer, and she's got too much sense."

"Is that so?"

Mr. French turned and cocked an eyebrow in Nicola's direction. Fortunately, since Nicola didn't know what to say, Mrs. French said it for her.

"Of course it is! No fourteen-year-old devotes herself to hours of hard work practicing every week just for the fun of it. It's not like stamp collecting or joining the Girl Scouts. You have to be pretty devoted, you know, to undergo the rigors of ballet training."

"Pretty insane, if you ask me." Mr. French winked at Nicola as he removed his coffee from the tray. "I'm afraid it's all a bit too high-powered for us lesser mortals. I shall make myself scarce and leave the lunatic fringe to get on with it."

"Right." Mrs. French spoke briskly. She patted the sofa. "Come and sit down, and let's talk. How much do you know about Kendra Hall?"

By the time she left, Nicola knew a great deal. She knew that it was up in London and that she would have to travel there every day either by bus or by train and then by subway. She knew that the Hall itself was an ancient manor house, that it had its own grounds where the pupils could play tennis or basketball (but not hockey, for fear of broken limbs), and that it had its own theater, where shows were put on every term.

"A beautiful little place—used to be stables in the old days. You'll love it. I know you will."

Mrs. French seemed every bit as excited as Nicola. She gave her an application form, which had to be signed by one of her parents. "Perhaps you could ask them tonight? The sooner we get it off, the better." She also gave her a copy of the brochure showing a picture of the Hall, with photographs of various classes and the names of all the staff and the subjects they taught. On the last page was a long list of pupils who had become famous, or at least well known. Under *F* it said, *Pamela French, former member of the Royal Ballet, now teaching.*

"Just think," said Mrs. French, "your name might be there one day. . . ."

Nicola thought about it all the way home, which actually wasn't very far as it was only a few hundred yards down the road, and most of that she covered in an exuberant series of *grands jetés,* leaping from crack to crack in the pavement. The family, including Ben, were all in the living room, snug with the electric heater turned on. Rose and Mrs. Bruce were sitting in front of the television watching their favorite soap opera, which was all about life backstage at a famous London theater. Every few seconds as they watched, Rose would shriek or groan or roll her eyes, just to demonstrate that she *knew* what life was like backstage and it wasn't like that. Mrs. Bruce would say consolingly that this was because the series was meant for "ordinary people," and not for dyed-in-the-wool professionals such as Rose.

"Ordinary people like to think they know what goes on, even if it is a bit exaggerated."

Mr. Bruce, who was as ordinary as could be and didn't care, was sitting in the corner smoking his pipe and reading one of his gardening books. Ben was the only one to look up as Nicola came in. He grinned and thumped her a welcome from the hearth.

"That was a long class," said Mrs. Bruce.

"It wasn't all class," said Nicola. "We were talking. I've got an application form for you to sign. It's for me to go to Kendra Hall."

"Kendra Hall?" Rose bounced around in her chair. "You'll never get into Kendra Hall!"

Some of Nicola's excitement fell away from her.

"How do you know?"

"They're ever so choosy—they never take anyone."

"They've got to take *some*one."

"A girl at Ida Johnson tried three times, and they didn't take her."

"So what?"

"So she was *really* good," said Rose.

"Obviously not good enough." Mrs. Bruce leaned forward and switched the television off. Rose let out a wail.

"Don't do that! I want to know what happens!"

"Well, you'll just have to wait till Monday. We can't talk with that thing blaring away. Where's this application form I have to sign?"

"Here." Nicola pulled it out of the back pocket of her jeans, together with the brochure. "It's this bit where it says *consent of parent or guardian....* We've already filled in all the rest. All you have to do is just sign it, and then we can send it off."

"And then what happens?" That was Mr. Bruce from within his clouds of pipe smoke.

"Then they send her a date for an audition."

"And what happens if she's accepted?"

"Well, then they offer her an appointment, a place they call it."

"She won't be," said Rose. "People never are. Not unless they're progenies."

"Prodigies," said Mr. Bruce. "What sort of appointment are we talking about? Full-time, or —"

"Full-time, yes."

"You mean she'd have to leave Streatham?"

"Well, obviously!" Mrs. Bruce held out a hand. "Lend me your pen."

"Before you sign anything," said Mr. Bruce, "don't you think perhaps we ought to discuss it?"

"Discuss what? What is there to discuss?"

Mr. Bruce turned and knocked out his pipe. (Mrs. Bruce tutted crossly as some of the ash fell to the floor.)

"Isn't Nicola a bit young to be making this sort of decision?" Mr. Bruce said.

"At fourteen?" Nicola's mother replied. "On the contrary, I should say she's rather old."

"Fourteen's practically middle-aged," said Rose.

"Middle-aged!" Mr. Bruce laughed. "Will you listen to the child!"

Rose didn't like being laughed at, or being called a child. She tossed her hair back angrily.

"Well, it is! Most people start when they're only five."

"Exactly," said Mrs. Bruce. She reached for her handbag and began rooting through it in search of a pen of her own. "If Nicola doesn't decide now, she might just as well forget about it."

Mr. Bruce frowned.

"Are you seriously telling me that by the time she's old enough to leave high school, it would be too late?"

"As far as ballet is concerned, yes."

"So at the age of fourteen she's expected to make a decision that could affect the whole of the rest of her life?"

"It's a big chance," said Mrs. Bruce. "She can't afford not to take it. It's a question of now or never."

Mr. Bruce shook his head. Rose, who had sneaked forward and switched the television back on, with the volume turned down to escape attention, settled herself contentedly in front of it.

"Of course, you don't actually *have* to go when you're still young. Susie Siegenberg's sister didn't go till she was almost seventeen."

Nicola looked at Rose resentfully. Whose side was she on? (And who was Susie Siegenberg's sister anyway?)

"It's only people who are really dedicated who go as soon as they can."

"You can't be really dedicated at fourteen," said Mr. Bruce. "You're not old enough to know your own mind."

"I was!" shrilled Rose. "I was dedicated at only *nine!*"

"In any case"—Mrs. Bruce finally took her pen to the paper and put her bag back on the table—"the younger you start, the more chance you stand. If we'd discovered earlier that Nicola could dance, I'd have sent her to the Royal Ballet School when she was eleven. But of course we didn't realize—"

"It was her own fault," said Rose. "Always going around being the tomboy and playing soccer. She didn't even *like* ballet. She kept saying it was stupid."

Nicola, kneeling on the hearth rug scratching the inside of Ben's ear for him with her little finger, wondered if Rose really was as dumb as she sometimes seemed to be, or whether it was simply that she was so bound up in herself and her own concerns that she never bothered to stop and think about other people and what made them do some of the things that they did. Had she not figured out even yet that when Nicola had said ballet was stupid and had gone off to kick soccer balls, it had all been in self-defense, to comfort her wounded pride? Because when people called you things like Spiderman and Nicola Long Legs, and everyone said how gawky you were, how clumsy and awkward and uncoordinated, what could you do but act tough and pretend not to care? Of course, Rose probably wouldn't understand, because no one had ever said that Rose was clumsy or awk-

ward. Rose had always been the dainty, charming one. There hadn't been any need for her to go and kick soccer balls and pretend she was tough.

"What I want to know," said Mr. Bruce, "is what happens if she gets to this place and then, after a couple of years, she changes her mind? Suppose she suddenly decides she doesn't want to be a dancer after all? Then what do we do?"

Mrs. Bruce looked at him in exasperation.

"You didn't say that about Rose!"

"Oh, well, Rose." Mr. Bruce hunched a shoulder, as if disclaiming all responsibility for Rose. "You'd already made the decision."

"Anyway," said Rose, "it's different for me. I couldn't do anything else."

Nicola knew that when Rose said she couldn't do anything else, she didn't mean she wasn't capable of doing anything else but that nothing on earth was ever going to make her. Rose was very single-minded. She told everybody that life wouldn't be worth living if she couldn't get up on the stage and act. "I'd rather *die*," she had said. Nicola wouldn't rather die. She thought that was a bit silly and melodramatic, which probably just went to show that she wasn't as dedicated as Rose. In fact, now that she came to think about it, she quite obviously wasn't. Rose would never dream of going to soccer matches, or playing hockey, or reading books that weren't about the theater. She would have considered it a waste of time. Perhaps she was right, and it was "different for her."

All the same, it wasn't every day you were given the opportunity to audition for a place like Kendra Hall, and dedication or not Mrs. French seemed to think she stood a chance. She couldn't understand why her father was making all these objections. Usually he just went along with whatever Mrs. Bruce said, especially when it had to do with education.

"She got it!" said Rose. She sat back on her heels in disgust, in front of the television. "Cora got the part! That's *stupid*. She'd never have gotten it in real life. In real life they'd just have told her to go away and do something else . . . that's really *stupid*."

"Turn the set off," said Mrs. Bruce.

"But I want to watch! It's *Magic Master*."

"I don't care what it is, turn it off."

"But I *said* I'd watch! One of the girls at Ida Johnson—"

"You heard what your mother said," said Mr. Bruce. "Turn it off."

Sulking, Rose did so. Nicola removed her finger from Ben's ear and held it out for him to inspect.

"The thing that bothers me," said Mr. Bruce, "is that Nicola's a bright girl—"

"So is Rose!"

"Not in the same way. Nicola's a real scholar. Look at that report card she had last half-term . . . A's in nearly everything."

Nicola was impressed. She hadn't known her father ever bothered to read her report card.

"She only got A's in English and biology," said Mrs. Bruce.

"Well, then, all A's and B's. Almost everyone, as I recall, said she was a good worker or showed great promise."

"She obviously shows great promise as a dancer,

too, or Mrs. French wouldn't be putting her up for the audition."

"They put up hundreds of people," said Rose.

"Then that's all the more reason, if she gets through, that she goes ahead and does it. You couldn't ask for much more confirmation than that ... being accepted by a school like Kendra Hall."

"It's not the Royal Ballet School," said Rose.

"It's not far off it! Don't you start getting jealous, my girl, just because you were no great shakes as a ballet dancer."

Wonders would never cease! Mrs. Bruce was actually *admitting* that Rose was no great shakes at something? It was quite true, looking back on it. Rose's *arabesques* had been decidedly wobbly, and her *pirouettes* had been all over the place. She had never had what Mrs. French called "line."

"I could've taken ballet," said Rose. "The only reason I didn't was Mrs. French said I had too many other talents, and it would be a shame to waste them."

Rose was always so *modest*, thought Nicola. She put her face close to Ben's so that they could touch tongues. Rose said that that was a disgusting thing to do. She said it was a wonder Nicola didn't contract some vile and ghastly disease.

"The point I'm trying to make," said Mr. Bruce, repacking his pipe, "is that Nicola also has other talents but that hers lie in a different direction. She ought at least to be given the chance to take some advanced-level courses before being pushed into anything."

"We get to take advanced levels at Ida Johnson!" shrieked Rose.

"So do they at Kendra Hall," said Mrs. Bruce. "It says here" she read from the brochure—"*Pupils enter for general education examinations at the high school advanced level in the following subjects: arithmetic, French, English language, English literature, history, geography, human biology, art, and music.* I would think that would be enough to keep anyone happy."

"And what about that other thing she was talking of studying? Physics, chemistry, whatever it was?"

"You don't need physics and chemistry," said Mrs. Bruce, "to be a dancer." She removed the top from her pen and spread out the application form. "Nicola, stop slobbering over that dog and go and get an envelope. We'll send it off right away."

CHAPTER ❧ *Four*

"Nicola Tolstoy."

"Nicola *Mark*ova."

"Nicola Markova!" Cheryl slammed down her loose-leaf notebook triumphantly. "That sounds good! Why can't you be Nicola Markova?"

Nicola, perched on the window sill of her eighth-grade homeroom pretending to study the view, didn't bother pointing out that there had already been a dancer called Markova. She left that sort of thing to Janice Martin, who had taken ballet since she was eight years old and thought she was the world's leading authority. Sure enough, her voice came clanging across the room. "She can't be Markova. There's already been one!"

Cheryl, unmoved, tore open a bag of bacon-flavored chips and crammed a handful into her mouth.

"I've never heard of them."

"Never heard of Alicia *Mark*ova?"

"Never heard of *Nicola* Markova."

"I didn't *say* Nicola Markova."

"Anyway," said Nicola, "I'm not having a stage name."

Cheryl turned and looked at her reproachfully.

"Dancers always have stage names!"

"Not always."

"They do if they're English."

"Like Margot Fonteyn." That was Janice Martin again, showing off. She was going to tell them all how Margot Fonteyn had started life as Peggy Hookham. "*She* started off as Peggy Hookham."

"Anyone would change their name if they were called Peggy Hookham," said Nicola. Across the yard came a group of boys. She strained to see if one of them was Denny, but it wasn't, it was Suresh Patel from the homeroom down the hall.

"It's got to be something Russian," said Sarah.

"Barishnikov."

"Ulanova—"

Nicola turned back to the window. She hoped Denny arrived before classes started. She wanted to tell him about the audition. She had told Sarah at the school gates, and already the news had spread around half the eighth grade, the female half. (The male half remained steadfastly unimpressed.) But it was Denny she really wanted to tell.

"Nicola Shostakovich."

"Nicola Tchaikovsky."

"Nicola Rimsky-Korsakov."

"You ought to have a name ready," said Sarah. "Then you can be known by it right from the start."

Nicola frowned and wrapped one leg around the

other. They all seemed to be assuming that simply because she'd been put up for an audition, she'd as good
as been offered a place. It was going to make it all the
more difficult when she failed to get in. *If* she failed to
get in. Rose didn't know everything. Mrs. French
thought she stood a chance.

From inside the supply closet, where she was self-
importantly counting paper clips in her role as supply monitor, came Linda Baker's voice, somewhat
muffled. She seemed to be saying, "Doan cown chinz."
There was a pause.

"Don't *what?*" said Sarah.

"Doan cown chinz," said Linda. *Crash.* That was
the box of paper clips falling down. Serves her right,
thought Nicola. Anyone who would bother counting
paper clips every day needed her head examined.
"Mikezun*anj*ler"—scrabble, scrabble on hands and
knees—"three gole *mells.*"

"Really?" said Sarah. She sounded rather bored.
They had been hearing about Linda Baker's cousin
Angela and her three gold medals ever since elementary school. "Just because *she* didn't get in doesn't
mean Nicola won't."

And as for counting chickens—was *that* Denny?—
it was the last thing she was likely to do. Nobody
could count chickens with Rose around.

"Talent runs in families," said Cheryl. (No, it
wasn't Denny. She bet the lazy pig had gone and
overslept.) "Like that Miranda girl that played the
cello and had a sister that did it as well."

Someone said, "What's that got to do with anything?"

"Well, it's like Nicola taking ballet and having a sister that's at stage school. It's talent running in families."

From inside the closet came what sounded like a snort. Janice Martin—who everybody knew was jealous because she'd been at Madam Paula's the same as Rose had, the only difference being that Rose had gotten somewhere and she hadn't—flicked back her single, solitary mouse-colored pigtail and said, "Stage school! Anyone can get into *stage* school. You don't need talent for that sort of thing."

Nicola turned from her watcher's position at the window.

"What sort of thing?"

"Well—" Janice waved a hand. "Dreamy Liquid ... I ask you!"

"That's commercials," said Nicola. "She only does them for the money. Anyone would."

"*I* wouldn't," said Janice.

Nicola sniffed.

"You wouldn't get the opportunity." Rose might be absolutely foul, but Nicola wasn't having some great, useless, flabby creature like Janice Martin run her down. At least Rose was good at what she did. When she'd played Amy in *The March Girls*, at a real West End theater, *The Stage* had said that she was "pert, pretty, and altogether irresistible." Nobody could say that of Janice Martin.

"Thing is"— Cheryl stuffed her last few bacon-flavored chips into her mouth and scrunched up the empty bag—"even when she does Dreamy Liquid, she's got *something*. I don't know what it is, and whatever it is"—the scrunched-up bacon-chip bag flew through the air, landing yards away from its objective, which was the wastepaper basket—"whatever it is, it's absolutely *yucky*, but then it's *supposed* to be yucky. Children in ads are *always* yucky. It's what people like. It's just that Rose manages to be more yucky when *she* does it than anybody else."

"That's *right.*" Sarah nodded. "Like when she played that *really* yucky part in the West End."

"*Aimee.*"

Somebody said, "Vomit, vomit!" and clutched at her stomach. Several people obligingly made vomiting noises. They could laugh, thought Nicola, but they'd all gone along to see the show and had been happy enough to be taken backstage afterward to visit Rose in her dressing room. Some of them had even asked her to sign autograph books—for their little sisters, so they *said.* Linda Baker, who didn't have a little sister, had actually unblushingly claimed it was for her mother.

"Hey!" Sarah suddenly poked at her. "There's your boyfriend!"

Nicola, taken unaware, spun around. (She always intended to remain very calm and offhand and not to respond when people referred to Denny as her boyfriend, because only let them think for one moment that things might be serious and they tended to get silly and start on the stupid jokes and ho-ho-look-who's-coming routine.)

"Who are you talking to?" she said, but she had waited too long.

Sarah grinned and wagged a finger.

"*We* know who you went to the soccer match with . . . *we* saw you walking down High Street together."

Honestly! Nicola shook her head crossly. It seemed there was no privacy to be had anywhere in this town. If it wasn't Rose spying on her from the window of a bus, it was Cheryl and Sarah peering goggle-eyed through the windows of the Treat Shop.

Denny was ambling across the field as if he had all the time in the world instead of a mere sixty seconds before the bell rang for homeroom roll call.

"Did you want him?" said Sarah. Before Nicola could stop her, she had flung open the window and was leaning out, shouting. "Hey you! Lover Boy ... your sweetheart's waiting!"

Denny stopped and looked up. As he did so, Miss Camfield, who was their homeroom teacher, passed beneath the window. She, also, stopped and looked up.

"Sarah Mason," she said, "what are you doing leaning out of that window screaming like a wild woman?"

Sarah withdrew, giggling. Under cover of the general rush to get to the window (everyone being anxious not to miss out on the fun), Nicola made good her escape. She bumped into Denny as he was halfway up the stairs. He jerked his head in the direction of the homeroom.

"What's all that about?"

"It's only Sarah—don't worry. Nobody takes any notice of her. Listen, I've—"

"What's she going on like that for?"

"*I* don't know, I s'pose she thinks it's funny. It's pitiful, really. People are so childish. Why are you late? I wanted to talk to you. I've got something to—"

"Nicola Bruce and Dennis Waters!" Miss Camfield had caught up with them. "What are you doing, idling in the corridor? Didn't you hear the bell? Stop chitter-chattering and get to your homeroom."

"Listen," hissed Nicola, "I'm going to have an *audition.*"

"Audition for what?"

"Ballet school."

"What ballet school?"

"Kendra Hall."

"What's that?"

"Did you hear what I said?" said Miss Camfield.

Nicola put her hand over her mouth. "Tell you later."

"Nicola Bruce! How long have you been at this school? Long enough to know the rules—and you, young man, just get a move on! Whatever it is, it will have to wait. It can't be as important as all that."

Probably to Miss Camfield, an audition for ballet school wouldn't seem very important because Miss Camfield was their phys-ed teacher as well as their homeroom teacher, and as far as she was concerned, ballet was just a nuisance. It meant that every so often, when Nicola had a dancing test coming up and couldn't afford to run the risk of pulled ligaments or strained muscles, she would have to drop out of the field hockey or the girls' softball team, or the special gymnastics group, and a replacement would have to be found. Miss Camfield accepted the necessity, but it didn't stop her from grumbling.

"You girls and your wretched ballet dancing! Is it really worth it?"

Nicola knew that neither Denny nor Miss Camfield felt that it was, but she had thought that Denny, being Denny, might be just a *little* bit excited for her. Instead, when she finally managed to get him on his own—which wasn't easy in a school of eight hundred pupils, where spies lurked around every corner—all he said, rather grumpily, was "What's all this about ballet school?"

"I've got an audition! At least, I've applied for one."

"What for?"

"What d'you mean, what for?"

"What d'you want an audition for? You're already at a ballet school."

"Not a really good one. Mrs. French only takes a few pupils, Kendra Hall's full-time. I'd be having classes every day!"

"*Ballet* classes?" Denny sounded incredulous. "Every *day?*"

She nodded earnestly.

"You have to, if you're going to be a dancer."

"Thought you were going to be a doctor and go to India."

"That was only if I didn't study ballet. I still might, if I don't get in—which I probably won't. Not many people do. I don't really expect I stand much chance. Mrs. French thinks I might, but"—she gave a little laugh, just to show she wasn't boasting—"I don't expect I will."

"So what're you bothering to try for?"

"Well, I *might*. Mrs. French thinks I might. She wouldn't put just anybody up. She only puts you up if she thinks you're good enough."

"Yeah, but if you don't think you are—"

"I think I'm *quite* good." She just didn't know how good. That was the whole point of taking the audition, so that she could find out. She said so to Denny, who looked glum.

"Don't know why you want to be good at a stupid thing like that anyway."

"It's not stupid!" She was indignant. Why was he being so nasty all of a sudden?

"Crazy thing to do," said Denny. He picked up a stone and flung it, with some force, toward the bicycle sheds, where it landed with a clunk on someone's back fender. Nicola winced. Denny was obviously in a bad mood. She wondered what had happened to upset him. "Standing around on one leg like a stupid bird."

"It's not only just standing around on one leg! It's learning how to control your body, so that you can do things with it."

"Yeah, like wriggling around on stage on your stomach, pretending to be a snake."

Nicola flushed. That wasn't fair. That had been Mr. Jordan's idea for last year's Christmas play—the Garden of Eden, with Nicola as the serpent, all rolled up in a luminous green body stocking that had encased even her legs. People had called her Snake Eyes for weeks afterward.

"That wasn't ballet—you know it wasn't! You're just saying that to be cruel."

Denny scowled and flung another stone.

"And you shouldn't do that," said Nicola. "You'll break something."

"Do it if I want."

He threw another, just to prove it. Nicola regarded him for a moment, exasperated. It was not like Denny to be so mean. She couldn't understand why he was doing it. An idea suddenly struck her.

"You know that math test we had this morning?"

"Mmm."

"I only got four out of ten."

Denny grunted.

"What did you get?" said Nicola.

"Ten." He said it aggressively, as if she should have known better than to ask. Denny always got ten, or at the very least nine. It would be a bad day if he got any less.

Well, he hadn't gotten any less, so that wasn't it. She racked her brains for something else.

"Has Frank Woolgar been on your case again?"

"No, why?"

"Just wondered."

"I'll punch his head in for him," said Denny, "next time he tries it."

"Punching heads doesn't do any good."

"Does with idiots like that."

Nicola pursed her lips. Talking to Denny in this mood was impossible. She didn't know why she bothered. He wasn't making the slightest bit of effort; and even if something *had* happened to upset him (though it was difficult to imagine what), she still didn't see that this was any reason for him to be such a beast.

"There's your sister," she said.

Denny looked up and made a noise that sounded like *"Humph!"* Then he looked back down again and kicked a stone.

"She should have taken ballet." Denny's sister was sixteen, and in tenth grade. She was tall and athletic, with long, strong legs that were made for running—or

for turning *pirouettes* or doing *grands battements.* "I
bet she'd be good at it."

"What's she want to take ballet for? She's gonna be
a nurse."

"Why a nurse?" Nicola pounced on it instantly.
Miss Richardson, this term, had been talking to them
about role playing. (She had thought at the time it
was a pity that Denny wasn't there to profit by it.)
"Why a nurse and not a doctor?"

"*I* dunno." Denny hunched a shoulder. "Never
asked her."

"Girls always choose to be nurses. It's like girls
being stewardesses and secretaries and *house*wives.
You don't see men becoming any of those things—
well, sometimes you do, but not very often."

"So what?" said Denny.

"So it's role playing," said Nicola.

Denny jeered, "Women's lib garbage!"

Nicola felt her face grow hot and prickles break out
all along her spine.

Denny at least had the grace to look a bit ashamed.
He scuffed a toe in the moth-eaten grass that bordered
the playing field.

"Anyway," he said, "you need brains to be a doctor."

"Your sister's got brains!" Denny's sister had
reached highest honors levels, which was more than
Denny was likely to reach unless he started working a
bit harder at some of those subjects he claimed to de-
spise, such as English and French. "I bet she could
get to college as easy as pie."

"Bet you could, too," said Denny.

"Yes, but it's different for me." (Horrors! she

thought. Echoes of Rose . . .) "I mean, I don't *know*
that I could get into college, whereas if I *did* get into
Kendra Hall—not that I expect I *will*, but if I *did*—"

"You could always turn it down," said Denny.

She stared at him, shocked.

"I couldn't do that!"

"Why not?"

"Well, because—because I *couldn't*. People *don't*.
It'd be like turning down the Nobel Prize, almost."

Denny looked at her. She colored slightly.

"Well, perhaps not *quite* like that."

"It's only a ballet school."

"Yes, I know."

"It's not like working for peace or discovering a
cure for cancer."

"I *know*. I didn't mean that. All I meant was that
lots of people try to get in and hardly anybody does,
so that if you're one of the ones that's chosen—well, it
means you've got to be *some* good. And if you're good
at something, and it's something that's—" She sought
for a word and couldn't find it. "If it's something that
people like and it doesn't do any harm, well, then, I
think you *ought* to do it, almost." Denny looked at her
again. She hurried on before he could say anything.
"That's why I think your sister ought to be a doctor,
because she'd be good at it and because there aren't
many women doctors and *I* think there ought to be
more of them. Especially *black* women doctors. I bet
there probably aren't any black women doctors in this
country at all, hardly. That's another reason why she
should do it. It's important for people to set examples"—that was what Miss Richardson had said—

"especially when people are oppressed, like women and —"

"My sister's not oppressed," said Denny.

"*Women* are oppressed, and *black* people are oppressed, and —"

"You know something?" said Denny. "You're starting to sound like Frank Woolgar."

Nicola tossed her head.

"I'd rather sound like Frank Woolgar than a male chauvinist pig! At least Frank Woolgar *thinks.*"

"Thinks a load of rubbish."

"It isn't rubbish! Not all of it. Some of it is"—like saying Denny shouldn't go out with her; that was rubbish—"but not everything. I mean, fighting for a cause . . . people *ought* to fight for causes."

"Well, I'm not." Denny stated it fiercely. "I'm not fighting anything for no one, and 'specially not for people who go around trying to lay down the law about what other people ought to do." Nicola wasn't sure whether he was referring to her or to Frank Woolgar—to both of them, perhaps. "I'm not fighting no wars, and I'm not fighting for no causes, and I'm not—"

She never discovered what else Denny wasn't going to fight, because at that point there was an interruption. The bushes behind them suddenly erupted, and Sarah and Cheryl burst through.

Sarah said, "Oops! My apologies," and giggled.

Cheryl said, *"So* sorry. Didn't know you were here," and also giggled. Denny glowered at them as if they were something nasty that had crawled out of a dunghill.

"What d'you two want?"

"Oh! Pardon me, I'm sure." Cheryl clapped a hand to her mouth, stifling another burst of giggles. "We didn't realize anything *important* was going on."

"Had we realized," said Sarah, "we would never have materialized."

"Certainly *not.*"

"It would absolutely never have occurred to us."

"Abso*lutely.*"

"If we'd known you were having a *summit* meeting—"

"Why don't you just shut up?" said Denny.

He stalked off across the field. Sarah stared after him.

"What's his problem?"

Don't know, thought Nicola. Wish I did.

"He doesn't like people spying on him," she said.

"*Spy*ing?"

"*Us?*'

"Yes, you," said Nicola. "You're just about the limit, you two."

CHAPTER ✿ Five

On Saturday Rose had her party. It didn't start until six o'clock in the evening, which seemed an odd time, but Rose wouldn't have it in the afternoon. She said that afternoon parties were all right for ordinary people, who went to ordinary schools, but "in the profession" people didn't really come alive until after midnight.

"Well, you're certainly not having a party that goes on till midnight," Mrs. Bruce had said.

"*After* midnight. We really shouldn't start until nine o'clock."

"Rubbish! You'll start at six and finish at eight-thirty. That's quite late enough."

"Well, so long as we can have a buffet supper," said Rose.

"What do you mean, a buffet supper? What's the matter with a sit-down meal?"

Everything, it seemed, was the matter with a sit-down meal. A sit-down meal was for children and ordinary people. It had been quite all right when Rose was small, but not now that she was *thirteen*. She screeched with horror when Mrs. Bruce suggested ice cream and candies and a birthday cake with pink icing.

"Not for a buffet supper!"

"Then what sorts of things do you want?"

Mrs. Bruce had seemed baffled. As a rule, she and Rose understood each other very well (far better than she and Nicola, who scarcely ever saw eye to eye at all), but on this occasion Rose had obviously jumped one step ahead. Mrs. Bruce had not yet had a chance to catch up. To her a birthday party was only a birthday party if there were balloons and cookies and funny hats—and, of course, ice cream and candies and a birthday cake with pink icing. Rose scoffed at the idea. What she wanted was a party like "the ones they have in the TV studios." Last year Rose had been in a television production of *Children of the New Forest,* and at the end of filming there had been a party for all the cast and the crew at which champagne had been served, and lobster patties, and sausages on sticks. That was the sort of thing she wanted.

Mrs. Bruce, for once, had stood firm. Lobster was out of the question, and so was champagne. She didn't care if Rose *had* drunk it at the television party. She didn't care if all Rose's little friends at Ida Johnson were in the habit of guzzling it down like tap water. They were not going to do any guzzling at Number 10 Fenning Road.

"I'm not having a horde of drunken thirteen-year-olds staggering around the place."

Rose had grumbled and said that everyone would

think they were stingy. She had said she wasn't having orange soda because orange soda was too childish for words, and why couldn't she pay for lobster patties out of her own money, which she had earned?

"It's cruel eating lobsters," said Nicola. "They put them in boiling water while they're still alive."

"You shut up!" cried Rose. "It's no crueler than eating anything else!"

"Yes, it is."

"No, it isn't!"

"Yes, it *is.*"

"No, it isn't. What about cows? They kill *them* while they're still alive, don't they?"

Nicola fell silent. She wondered why it was that whenever she argued with Rose she always seemed to lose. Mrs. Bruce did somewhat better by the simple method of exercising parental authority. She said that Rose was not frittering away her earnings on lobster patties and that was that.

At this Rose had gone into a tremendous sulk and had threatened to tell everyone that the party had been canceled. "And what's more, I'll tell them it's because of you! Because you're too mean and stingy to let me spend my own money!"

"You can tell them what you like," said Mrs. Bruce.

"I will! I'll tell them you've suddenly gone nuts and been taken to a mental hospital!"

"I probably will go nuts and be taken to a mental hospital," said Mrs. Bruce, "if there's very much more of this."

For a day or two it had looked as though there wasn't going to be any birthday party. Nicola told Denny that it had probably been called off, and

Denny said good, that meant they could go to the cin-
oma instead and see *Wars of the Thirty-Ninth Gal-
axy*. They had almost definitely arranged it when
Rose and Mrs. Bruce reached a compromise. There
was still not going to be any champagne, but they
could have some bottles of sparkling apple juice,
chilled in the refrigerator, and if Rose wanted to pretend it was champagne, then that was up to her. As
for lobster patties, said Mrs. Bruce, she could make
them with crab meat and no one would ever know the
difference.

"You can always tell them it's lobster, if that's what
you want."

"So long as *she* doesn't go and say anything." Rose
looked venomously at Nicola, who tossed her head.

"Why should I spoil your childish games?"

By six o'clock on Saturday the table in the front
room was all laid out with crab patties and sausages
on sticks. There were bowls of potato chips and salted
peanuts. There were dishes of stuffed olives and plate-
fuls of crackers spread with garlic butter, and cubes
of yellow cheese with bits of cucumber or salami
skewered onto them. Rose was happy and said those
were exactly the kinds of things her friends liked to
eat. Rose's friends must have very peculiar tastes—
that was all Nicola could say. She had sampled little
bits of things as she helped carry trays in from the
kitchen, and the only things that were any good were
the potato chips and salted peanuts and the sausages
on sticks. The garlic butter was foul, the cucumbers
were all sour and watery, and the salami was full of
fatty, white lumps. She couldn't eat the crab patties

because crabs, like lobsters, were plunged into boiling water. The olives were slimy and tasted like snot, and the stuffing was so hideously and horribly hot that it almost took the roof of your mouth off. She would far rather have had ice cream and candies and birthday cake with pink icing any day of the week. She didn't care if they *were* ordinary and childish. She supposed that just went to show what Rose was so often telling her: "You haven't any sophistication whatsoever."

At ten past six the first group of guests arrived. They had met up at Victoria Station and traveled on the same train. Nicola could hear them coming when they were still only halfway down the road. Their voices, like Rose's, were peculiarly penetrating and shrill. Everybody had brought a birthday present. They were the sorts of presents that grown-ups gave each other—bottles of perfume, bubble bath, and the like. Nicola wouldn't have looked twice at them, but Rose appeared delighted, at any rate if her oohs and aahs were anything to go by.

"Susie, that's *super!* That's just what I *wanted* ... Isn't it *gorgeous?* Doesn't it smell *super?* I just can't *wait* to put some on."

On the other hand, Rose and her friends were always oohing and aahing, so perhaps it didn't mean anything. One girl had brought a pair of blue dangly earrings which needed pierced ears. She cried out in amazement when Rose said she'd never had her ears pierced.

"Haven't you? I had mine done *ages* ago."

Rose instantly became wild about having her ears pierced right away. Mrs. Bruce said, "We'll see. Perhaps for Christmas." Nicola could tell, from the expression on Rose's face—her lips were pursed so tight that they almost turned in on themselves—that she had not the least intention of waiting till Christmas. Christmas was eight long months off. When Rose said right away, she meant *now*.

At a quarter past six Denny arrived, and soon after that another bunch of Ida Johnson students, who had also come from Victoria Station but on a different train. There were twelve girls in Rose's class at Ida Johnson and twelve boys. Rose had invited all of the girls and four of the boys. Like Mrs. Bruce, she didn't really care very much for boys. The four she had invited struck Nicola as being rather silly. They had silly names, for a start. One was Anthony, one was Conrad, one was Wayne, and one was Alastair. Unlike Denny, who had come in Levis and a sweater, they were all wearing shirts, and pants with creases. Anthony even had a polka-dot bow tie. Probably all of the other boys in Rose's class were quite normal, ordinary sorts of boys who wore jeans and sneakers and kicked soccer balls. But then Rose wouldn't invite normal, ordinary sorts of boys. She would think they were rough and uncouth, as Mrs. Bruce did.

All the girls were pretty and loud, just like Rose. They all had very long, thick hair, either very straight as if it had been ironed, or very curly and bouncy, except for one girl who had a frizzy perm, like bits of wire, which she said had just been done for her by "Mr. Marcus." Everyone stood around saying, "Gosh, it's *super*," and, "Gosh, you are *brave*," and "Gosh, d'you think it'd suit *me?*" Nicola, who privately thought it looked hideous, was incensed when Mrs.

Bruce said, "That's exactly what Nicola needs to have done to hers, to give it a bit of body."

"Hope you don't," whispered Denny.

"You must be *joking*," said Nicola.

Mr. Bruce, who wasn't good at parties, had gone out and locked himself away in his shed with his handsaw and his electric drill and his old tobacco tins full of assorted nails. Ben, because his manners were bad and because he couldn't be trusted not to get up on his hind legs and help himself to sausages and crab patties, not to mention knocking over people's drinks every time he wagged his tail, had been banished to the kitchen with a fresh marrow bone. Mrs. Bruce hovered in the doorway, as if she couldn't quite make up her mind whether to go or whether to stay. Rose had introduced her as "my big sister," and everyone had laughed, including Mrs. Bruce, who had said, "Get away with you!" and looked pleased. Nicola was introduced as, "my *other* sister, who studies ballet." Someone said, "Are you going to be a dancer?"

"Don't know yet," said Nicola.

"Of course you are!" Mrs. Bruce bustled forward with another bottle of chilled apple juice. "She's got an audition at Kendra Hall."

"Yes, but I haven't *passed* it yet."

"Well, even if you don't . . . there are other places."

She wasn't sure that she would want other places—not if she failed Kendra Hall.

"I couldn't bear to do an *ordinary* job," said the person who had asked if she were going to be a dancer. "Could you?"

The question was addressed not so much to Nicola as to the room in general. There was a chorus of

"Ughs" and *"Yucks,"* and Rose's voice rose clear above the hubbub, "I'd sooner *die* than not be able to act." The first girl said, "Me *too,"* and all the rest nodded their heads and made vigorous noises of agreement. Nicola had heard the cry so often that it no longer made any impression on her. Denny, however, was obviously struck by it.

"That's crazy," he said.

Everyone stopped nodding and turned to look at him.

"Typical," said the girl with the frizzy perm. "Absolutely *typical."*

"It's what comes of not being in the business," said Rose. (She and her friends and Mrs. Bruce always referred to the theater as "the business." It was either "the business" or "the profession.") "Ordinary people just don't understand."

"Don't understsnd what?" said Denny.

"That once you've been in it, there's literally *nothing* else that you can do."

"Nothing," said the girl with the frizzy hair.

A ripple of irritation passed across Denny's forehead.

"That's a lot of bull," he said.

"It's not bull!" The girl with the frizzy hair was beginning to bristle. "It's what's called dedication."

"I don't call it dedication," said Denny. "I call it stupid. Saying there's nothing else you can do. There's always *something* people can do."

"Like what?"

"Like washing dishes. Anyone could do that."

"I'd rather *die!"* said Rose.

"Bet you wouldn't," said Denny. "Not if it came to

it. I bet if it came to it, and someone said all right, I'll stick a needle in you, and then you can die sooner'n wash dishes, I bet you'd sooner wash dishes. Sooner'n let 'em stick a needle in you."

"I wouldn't *have* to let them." Rose made the statement grandly, in her best dramatic fashion. "There wouldn't be any need. If I couldn't act," said Rose, "I would already *be* dead without anyone sticking needles in me."

The girl with the frizzy hair said, "That's *it.*"

"So there!" said Rose.

Nicola wondered yet again why it was that Rose always seemed to have the last word. Even when you knew she wasn't right, you could never think of a comeback—not, at any rate, until hours later, when you'd unraveled all the strands of the argument and discovered where it was that she had hoodwinked you.

After the buffet supper had been demolished, and everyone had said how super the lobster patties were and how champagne was the most gorgeous drink in the world, Rose, in her bossy way, announced that they were all going to play Charades and that she and Frizzy Hair (who turned out to be Susie Siegenberg, the girl who thought she was a second Barbra Streisand and who suffered from terrible raging jealousy) were going to pick up teams. Denny and Nicola, because nobody knew them, were the last to be picked, which meant that they weren't together. Rose had Denny, because "I can't pick my own *sister,*" and Susie Siegenberg had Nicola.

"Nicola's good at mime," said Rose.

It wasn't very often that Rose handed out the compliments. Nicola felt a glow of pride and then felt cross with herself. It was only *Rose*. Still, even if it were only Rose, it would be nice to show all these screaming friends of hers that other people besides themselves could do things. She heard Denny saying that he didn't know what the game was about and Rose saying impatiently that he could pick it up as they went along. Then she was swept off into a corner with the rest of her team to think up phrases for the other side to mime.

"They've all got to be theatrical," said Susie.

Nobody disputed that, so Nicola didn't bother arguing—even though she'd just thought of a phrase that wasn't theatrical but that would have been nice to give Rose—"a pig in a poke." She would like to see Rose mime a pig. Someone said, *"The Mousetrap,"* and someone else said, *"Midsummer Night's Dream."*

"Puss in Boots."

"Babes in the Wood."

They managed to think of eight and then got stuck.

"What about Rumpelstiltskin?" said Nicola.

"That's not theatrical!"

"It is, sort of."

"No, it's not. It's a fairy tale."

"Yes, but it would be fun. You could do rumple, like rumpling hair, and stilt, like walking on stilts, and —"

"Hamlet," said Susie. "That'll do. I'll tell them we're ready."

Once, a long time ago, before she had started ballet with Mrs. French, Nicola had almost been in a mime show, playing the part of a Bad Little Girl. She *would* have been in it if it hadn't been for Rose. Rose had screamed and yelled almost nonstop for a whole week,

until in the end the part had had to be taken away
from Nicola and given to Rose instead. This was something that Nicola had never forgotten, but in spite of
that, she still enjoyed doing mime.

When it came to her turn, she was given *Simple
Spymen,* which Rose said was the title of a play,
though Nicola had never heard of it. Nicola turned to
her side, who had to do the guessing.

"Title of play: two words."

That was as much as she was allowed to say. All the
rest had to be acted out in mime. She held up one finger to show that she was about to mime the first word,
"simple." Simple was simple. She simply drooped her
head, stuck her thumb in her mouth, and turned in
her toes. Everybody laughed.

The boy called Wayne said, "Nutty!"

Nicola shook her head.

"Stupid?"

"Slow?"

"Half-wit?"

It wasn't long before someone hit on the correct
word. She nodded to show that they could stop guessing. Now she had to do "spymen." She decided to
break it into syllables. First she made chopping motions on her right arm with the fingers of her left
hand, which was the sign that meant "breaking into
syllables." Then she held up two fingers to indicate
that there were two of them.

"Spy" was easy. She opened an imaginary door,
glanced furtively this way and that, checking that the
coast was clear, slipped inside (taking care to close
the door very quietly behind her), crept on tiptoe
down some steps, knelt at the bottom, and peered with

one eye through an imaginary keyhole. Two or three people shouted "Spy!" almost immediately.

"Men" was a bit more difficult. She could have done the classical mime that Mrs. French had taught her, simply running the flat of her hand down her face and bringing it to a point to indicate a beard, which was what you did in ballet, but that would have seemed like cheating and anyway wasn't very inventive. She wondered for a moment if she dared do something rude and naughty, but thought she'd better not (Mrs. Bruce had come to watch), and before she could think of anything else, Susie Siegenberg had shouted *"Simple Spymen!"* and it was over.

"One minute thirty seconds," said Rose, who was timing them with her new birthday watch, which was digital and had lots of clever gadgets such as an alarm bell, a timer, and a calendar. "That means your side's taken twenty minutes and ten seconds in all. Ours has taken eighteen and one to go. So if we get the last one in less than two minutes and ten seconds, we've won and we get the prize."

"What prize?" said Nicola. She hadn't heard anything about prizes.

Rose looked around slyly at Mrs. Bruce.

"Everyone who's on the winning team gets a glass of sherry."

Mrs. Bruce raised an eyebrow. Rose sometimes *was* allowed a sip of sherry as a special treat (Nicola didn't care for it), but a sip was not quite the same thing as a glass. Rose was testing, seeing how far she could go, trusting her mother not to say no in front of people.

"Maybe just a thimbleful," said Mrs. Bruce.

Honor was satisfied. Rose turned back, triumphant, to her team.

"Two minutes nine seconds, and not a second more!"

It was unfortunate that the burden of being last should fall on Denny. Nicola could see, just looking at him, that he had already gotten all stiff and shy.

The mime he was given was *The Mousetrap.*

"Play." Denny announced stolidly. "It's got two words and the first one's 'the.' "

Squeals from his own side, howls of rage from the other.

"You're not allowed to *say!*"

"You have to make a sign for 'the,' " said Nicola. She doubled her fist. "Like that."

Mutinously Denny stuck out his lower lip. He doubled his fist. Rose said, *"The,"* and then added, "Now do the second word," all pompous and schoolmarmish as if he were a child. Denny rolled an anguished eye at Nicola. Obligingly she made chopping motions on her arm. Susie Siegenberg screeched, "Don't help him, don't help him!" and Mrs. Bruce, over by the door, said sharply, "Nicola! That's not fair."

Nicola sat back, disgruntled. What did she mean, not fair? What wasn't *fair* was expecting Denny to get up and play a game he'd never played before in front of a roomful of people who all went to stage school and had egos the size of giant balloons. No wonder he wasn't doing it right. People who enjoyed showing off never seemed to realize what an ordeal it was for people who didn't.

Denny, having reluctantly made chopping motions to indicate that he was breaking his word into syllables, was now, even more reluctantly, acting out the first one, jumping across the room with his hands held up in front of him. His team was plainly puzzled.

"Kangaroo," said Rose.

Nicola's team exploded. Nicola said, "Kangaroo's not a syllable," but no one took any notice of her. Denny went on jumping, and his team went on guessing.

"Jackrabbit?"

"Rabbit."

"Elephant!"

Denny, goaded, said, "Elephants don't jump."

"No talking!" screamed Susie Siegenberg.

Rose was growing cross.

"If you can't do the first one, you'd better go on to the second—and do it *properly.*"

"I am doing it properly!"

"You're not—you keep talking."

Denny scowled.

"Honestly," said Rose, "you can always tell when people are amateurs."

"Now, now," said Mrs. Bruce, "none of that—we can't all be talented." To Denny, kindly, she said, "Don't let them upset you. You just go on and do it in your own way."

Denny's idea of miming the word "trap" was hardly very inspired, Nicola had to admit. All he did, awkwardly because he was self-conscious, was leap in the air and clap his hands together. He did it so fast that his team was left blinking.

"What's that supposed to be?" said Rose angrily.

Denny opened his mouth.

"Don't talk!"

"Do it again."

"And do it so we can *see*."

For a second time Denny leaped into the air and clapped his hands together. Susie Siegenberg and one or two others started giggling. Rose, red in the face, shouted, "You're not *doing* anything!" Someone said, "He's jumping again," and even some of Denny's own team collapsed into giggles.

"But what's it supposed to *be?*"

"That's what you're supposed to be finding out," said Nicola.

"Do something else! Do it in a different way!"

Denny did try. He got down onto his knees and crawled about the carpet, then suddenly clamped his hand over a bright red flower that was part of the pattern. Someone said, "Kill!"

"Bang."

"Squash."

"Flat."

"Time!" Susie Siegenberg gave a shrill screech of triumph. "Two minutes and eleven seconds. That means we've won!"

Rose, deprived both of her sherry and the honor and glory, was by now bright scarlet.

"That's what comes of using amateurs. They're just so stupid. I *loathe* them."

There were times when Nicola felt so ashamed of being related to Rose that it almost hurt. Mrs. Bruce had already gone out to the kitchen to fetch the promised thimbleful of sherry for the winning side, or she might at least have made Rose apologize. Everyone said that Mrs. Bruce spoiled Rose, but even she wouldn't tolerate rudeness to guests.

Nicola left her seat and went over to Denny.

"Want to come and take Ben for a walk?"

Denny shrugged a shoulder.

"Can if you like."

"It'd be better than staying here," said Nicola.

As they reached the door, Rose's voice came shrieking after them, "Where are you two going?"

"Mind your own business," said Nicola.

In the hall they bumped into Mrs. Bruce, bearing a tray with six tiny, little glasses and three eggcups filled with sherry.

"It's all right," she said. "I've got everything. Who won in the end?"

"We did," said Nicola. "But I don't want any sherry. We're going to take Ben out."

"But the party isn't finished yet."

"Don't care," said Nicola. "Don't want to stay anymore."

For a moment she thought her mother was going to start lecturing her on bad manners ("Walking out of your own sister's birthday party!"), but she only shook her head and said, "Well, don't go too far. I want you back here before it's dark—and don't go to the park!"

They collected Ben from the kitchen and went out around the side of the house.

"Where we going?" said Denny.

"Anywhere." Anywhere that took them away from ghastly Rose. "Let's go to your place and show Ben to your mother."

"All right."

For a long while they walked in silence, the only sounds being the happy snuffling of Ben's nose as he investigated smells along the way. Nicola was still feeling too embarrassed for conversation. Sometimes, like when she saw Rose on stage, she felt almost proud to have her for a sister; other times, like now, she felt she would do anything to have a sister that was plain and quiet and ordinary, and *didn't* run around shrieking and making noise and always having to be the center of attention. Obviously Denny didn't feel much like talking either, because it wasn't until they reached Wentworth Road that he said anything.

"I s'pose," he said glumly, "you'll get like that when you go to this ballet school."

Nicola didn't ask him what he meant by "like that." She knew well enough.

"I certainly will *not*," she said, and then added as an afterthought, "Anyway, I haven't gotten there yet."

CHAPTER ✤ *Six*

The audition had been set for April 24, which was the week after Easter. The half-term ended ten days earlier, on April 14, with the usual flurry of midterm exams and sports competitions. Streatham had four sections, each of which was named after a particular color. Nicola was in Red, whose color was a nice bright scarlet. Blue's was wishy-washy navy, Yellow's was egg-sick and pale, and Green's was like pea puke. Last year she had played left wing for her section's under-fourteen field hockey team, which had swept the board, beating all the others in every game. This year she was supposed to have been playing for the under-fifteens and at the beginning of the term had even been elected captain, but Miss Camfield, quite nicely but nonetheless firmly, had said she didn't think it was a good idea to have a captain who might not always be available to play, so Linda Baker had ended up doing it instead. Now Miss Camfield was justified because in this, the most crucial match of all, the intersectional final between Red and Green, Nicola had to drop out and give way to the reserve. Miss Camfield shook her head and said that of course she understood, but it really did seem a shame when Nicola had worked so hard and the team had been doing so well.

"In my experience it's always fatal to break up a winning team. It upsets the whole balance. Still, if it's really important—"

She looked at Nicola hopefully as she spoke. Just for a moment Nicola was tempted. It *was* important; certainly it was important. It was the most important event of her life so far. On the other hand there was still almost two weeks to go, and she wasn't *very* likely to sustain any ghastly injury just playing a game of hockey. Janice Martin last year had admittedly tripped and broken her ankle, which had meant having her foot in a cast for weeks on end, but then Janice Martin was the clumsy sort of person who did things like that. Nicola wasn't clumsy.

"I suppose you couldn't possibly . . . "

Miss Camfield let the words trail off. She knew that Nicola couldn't possibly. So in her heart of hearts did Nicola. If you were going to be a dancer, you had to make sacrifices. Nicola had accepted that a long time ago. It still didn't make it any easier to bear, having to sit on the sidelines and watch while Janice Martin played left wing in her place. Janice Martin had improved since last year, when she had been clumsy enough to trip over her own feet. She actually made the pass that enabled Sarah, playing center forward, to score the winning goal. *That* made it even less easy to bear. Naturally she was glad that the Reds had won, but it was hard not to feel a pang as everyone rushed around congratulating Janice Martin when they could have been congratulating her. She had to remind herself very firmly that hockey was only a game, ballet was a vocation. Hadn't Rose and her mother told her so a million times? Unfortunately, when she heard Miss Camfield also congratulating Janice Martin ("If you play as well as that next year, you should make one of the school teams"), it didn't help as much as it probably should have. Horrid jealousy *would* persist in raising its head.

The midterm exam results were announced, and Nicola had an A-plus again in biology, A's in English and French, A-minus in music, B-plus in math and computer studies, C-minus in needlework, and was ranked third overall in the class.

"With marks like these," said Miss Camfield, "it does seem a terrible waste applying for ballet school."

Nicola spent the rest of the day thinking about it. It was true that dancers didn't *need* to be clever. Rose had never gotten A-plus on an exam in her life, although that was more through lack of interest than lack of what Miss Richardson called "gray matter." But equally there was no law that said dancers had to be stupid. She couldn't really see why it should be considered better to be a brilliant nuclear physicist than a brilliant ballet dancer. She said so to Denny as they walked home together that evening.

"It's 'cause nuclear physicists have to have brains," said Denny.

"Some dancers have brains."

"Yeah, but they don't actually have to use 'em," said Denny. "Not for dancing."

Nicola pondered a while.

"Don't see what's so wonderful about having brains anyway."

"Don't wear out like bodies."

"Yes, they do! Miss Richardson says your brain cells start dying the minute you're born."

"Yeah, but people can still use 'em," said Denny, "even when they're old. They don't get worn out by the time you're fifty, like legs and arms do."

That was true. Nicola thought of her grandfather, who could still read books and do his beloved crossword puzzles every day, even though his arthritis was so bad he could sometimes hardly walk. She wondered what Rose would do when she was as old as that and had arthritis. Sit in front of the TV, probably, watching videos of all her old shows and her commercials for Dreamy Liquid. She giggled.

"What you laughing at?" said Denny.

She told him of her vision of Rose. Denny took it seriously and said, "That's the sort of thing that happens when people don't have any brains."

"Rose has brains. She just doesn't use 'em."

"So that's what happens when people don't use 'em. You coming down to the club to play table tennis tonight?"

Nicola shook her head regretfully.

"I can't tonight. I've got an extra class with Mrs. French."

"What about tomorrow?"

"Tomorrow I've got to stay on at school; it's the dress rehearsal for the show."

Denny made a noise of disgust.

"S'pose you won't be able to come swimming on Saturday, either?"

"Not just before the show," said Nicola.

The Streatham spring show was always something special. This year it was even more special than usual, a punk-rock opera, composed by some senior music students, with the help of Mr. Forbes, who was the music director. Nicola had three solos to do. They all involved dancing, not singing, since she couldn't sing to save her life. They were not exactly the kinds of solos she had learned with Mrs. French, but maybe for that very reason they were all the more fun. The one she enjoyed most was the last one, where she dressed up as a punk marionette in in a garish wig of green and purple stripes. Everyone said that it was sure to bring the house down.

"What about the Saturday after?" said Denny. "S'pose you'll tell me you can't do it then 'cause of the audition?"

"It'll be all right *after* the audition." After the audition she would be able to do anything he wanted her to do—go swimming, play table tennis, even climb mountains, if he could find any for her to climb. "It's just that until that's over—"

"Until that's *over*," said Denny with heavy sarcasm, "I'm surprised you're even allowed to *walk*."

Rose couldn't come to the spring show because she was spending the weekend with Susie Siegenberg. She quite often spent weekends with Susie Siegenberg. Mrs. Bruce had once said, only half jokingly, that she didn't know why Rose didn't just pack her bags and go and live there. Susie Siegenberg, on the other hand, never spent weekends with Rose because, as Rose was forever explaining, the Siegenbergs' home was more exciting than the Bruces'.

"It's got a swimming pool, and a tennis court, and a room with a big screen for showing films. That's why it's best for me to go there."

Since Rose went there so often, it might have been thought that she could have postponed this one particular visit until the following week, but Mrs. Bruce didn't suggest it and Nicola wouldn't lower herself. When Rose, making her eyes get all big, said, "Gosh, I'm *really* sorry! I wouldn't have said I'd go if I'd realized," Nicola just shrugged her shoulders and pretended not to care.

"Doesn't matter—it's only some little school thing. Not professional."

"Yes, but even *so,*" said Rose.

There was a pause.

"I s'pose I could always phone Susie and tell her I can't come."

"Honestly," said Nicola, "it doesn't matter." She only said it because she knew that if she took her up on the offer, Rose would sulk inside herself and resent it. What Rose liked was to make magnanimous gestures without actually having to follow them through.

"But you are my *sister,*" said Rose.

"Well ..." Nicola hesitated. If Rose really did mean it, for once ...

"But then perhaps her parents might think it was a bit rude. I mean, accepting an invitation and then phoning to turn it down at the last moment. I promised I'd take my video of *Children of the New Forest*

for them. They never saw me in that. I said I'd take it
with me so we could watch it. I s'pose I could always
give it to Susie in class tomorrow. The only trouble is,
she's so forgetful. She'd probably leave it on the train
or something. I do feel *awful*. You should have reminded me earlier."

Rose shouldn't have needed any reminding. The
date had been circled in red marker on the kitchen calendar for weeks. There simply wasn't any excuse. Nicola would never have dreamed of not turning up for
one of Rose's performances. (There would have been
the most tremendous scene if she *had*.)

"Anyway," said Rose comfortably, "you're only
doing a couple of numbers."

"Three, actually," said Nicola.

"Yes, but I mean, it's not as if you're the star of the
show or anything. I mean, obviously I'd come *then*—
even if it did mean being rude to Susie's parents."

Oh, obviously, thought Nicola. Obviously, indubita-
bly, and without any doubt.

"It's not like when I was in *The March Girls*," said
Rose, growing happy. "I mean, I know I wasn't the
star, exactly, but it was in the West End, and I did
have my picture outside the theater, and I did have a
review in *The Stage*. D'you remember that review in
The Stage? What was it they said? Something about
Amy being irresistible."

Rose knew perfectly well what it was that *The
Stage* had said. Nicola wasn't going to pander to her
vanity by repeating it.

"Really," she said, "it was so long ago, I can't even
remember what you did in it."

"I sang that song! The Amy song! *How fine to be*

pretty." Rose promptly put on her Amy expression (a revolting simper) and began to do her little Amy dance around the room, singing lustily as she went, *"How fine to be pretty, and witty, and cute! How fine to be me—ah, me! A-my!* ... Surely you remember?"

Nicola made a vague, grudging, mumbling sound.

"You *must,"* said Rose. "I wore that plaid dress with the yellow sash. I've still got it upstairs. I'll go get it and show you. *Then* you'll remember."

Nicola comforted herself with the reflection that Rose was one of those people who was just naturally selfish. There probably wasn't anything she could do about it. It was like having pimply arms or thick ankles. If that was the way you were, then that was the way you were.

Even if Rose didn't come to the show, everybody else did. Mr. and Mrs. French came, and Denny and his family, and of course Nicola's own parents. Mr. Bruce wanted to know if he should bring earplugs or whether they would be provided. Nicola thought at first that he was being serious. It took her a moment or so to realize that he was only teasing.

"It's not as loud as all *that,"* she said.

The punk marionette number turned out to be a showstopper. It was called "Dance of a Lost Soul" and was funny but sad and serious, too, a fact that people obviously appreciated, because although at first they laughed, they gradually fell quite silent, not even coughing or shuffling or rustling their programs until the final moment of collapse, when the puppet master let the strings fall and the puppet slowly crumpled into a heap. Then the clapping started, slowly to begin with, but gathering momentum like a tidal wave. People clapped and clapped until their hands must have been sore.

Everyone, afterward, seemed to want to congratulate her. Miss Richardson came up, looking unusually attractive in a matching skirt and jacket, and a silk blouse with big floppy sleeves. Generally you only saw her in her white lab coat. She said, "That was excellent, Nicola! I knew you studied ballet, but I never realized you could dance like that."

Mr. French tapped his camera and told her, "Got some good ones here. You just wait till you see 'em!" Mrs. French, all smiles, said that it was fun to let your hair down occasionally. Mrs. Bruce kept explaining to perfect strangers, "that's my older daughter, the one that did the marionette dance. My younger one's at Ida Johnson. This one's got an audition at Kendra Hall."

Various members of the eighth-grade class rushed around shrieking, "Where's Nicola? Where's Nicola?" Sarah dragged her off to meet a cousin who was "mad about ballet and wants to talk to a real dancer. Cheryl could be heard yelling, "That's Nicola, over there. She's one of my two best friends!" Linda Baker, in her bossy, self-important fashion, wanted Nicola to "come and be introduced to my auntie." Even Janice Martin, who knew all there was to know, condescendingly allowed that the marionette dance had been "quite good."

"Not really *ballet*, of course, but quite good all the same."

A girl from eleventh grade came up and said, "That was great! It's about time we had some real talent in this place." The girl had never before said so much as a single word to Nicola, except perhaps to yell at her for talking when she shouldn't have or for not walking single-file when she should have. Even Miss Camfield, upset as she was about ballet taking priority over hockey and gym, had something nice to say. The only person who didn't was Denny. Denny didn't say anything at all for the simple reason that he wasn't there. She knew that he *had* been there because she had seen him sitting in the second row with his mother and sisters, but he didn't come backstage and was nowhere to be found in either the hall or the main corridor, where lots of people were still gathered. Surely, she thought, he couldn't be so mean as to have gone home without waiting for her?

Just for a moment all the lovely brightness threatened to cloud over, but then she turned and saw Mr. Forbes, the head of the music department. He was talking to Mr. Henry, the principal, and was nodding in Nicola's direction as he did so. Nicola caught his eye and quickly looked away, in case he thought that she was trying to eavesdrop.

"This is our young dancer." (They *had* been talking about her! They were coming toward her.) "Even did some of the choreography herself, from what I'm told."

"Really?" Mr. Henry beamed. "So she's a choreographer as well as a ballerina, eh?"

Nicola blushed and did her best to look modest. (She didn't want to correct Mr. Henry and tell him that "ballerina" was a special rank reserved only for the top few, like a prima donna in opera. It was funny how people seemed to think you could refer to any type of dancer, even the least important member of the ballet company, as a ballerina. They would never dream of calling an ordinary soldier a general.)

"A splendid job," said Mr. Henry. Someone from the local paper came, you know. I think there'll probably be a review. There'll *certainly* be one in the school paper. I can give you my word on that!"

Beaming and nodding, he went on his way, accompanied by Mr. French. Sarah, who had been hovering a few feet off, now came buzzing forward, all excited, to whisper, "I just heard Miss Camfield telling someone, 'That's the girl who's going to go to ballet school and be a dancer.' And the person she was talking to said, 'I'm not surprised—she's got a real touch of quality' . . . *Quality!*" Sarah gloated. "I bet no one ever said that about Rose."

They might have, thought Nicola, but anyway it wasn't as if she was in any sort of competition. She'd never wanted to be *better* than Rose.

"Nicola!" Her mother was beckoning to her, making signs that it was time to go. Nicola tore herself away with some reluctance. She could have stayed a lot longer, listening to all the comments (and receiving words of praise), but Mr. Bruce had had enough. He had never been a great one for going backstage or hanging around after a performance. Neither had Nicola in the old days, when it had been Rose who had been receiving all the praise. She wondered if that meant that deep down in the depths of herself, a realm she didn't know all that well, she was a really nasty, attention-seeking person. She didn't *think* that she was, but then Rose probably didn't think that she was vain and selfish either. It was only other people who thought so.

"Well!" said Mr. Bruce, as they left school by the main gates and turned toward High Street. "That was a turnup for the books."

Turnup for the books? What did that mean?

"A pity our Rosie wasn't there. It might have given her something to think about!"

"I do wish," said Mrs. Bruce, "that you wouldn't call her Rosie."

"What's a turnup for the books?" said Nicola.

"It means your father was pleasantly surprised. I keep telling him it's right for you to go to ballet school. Now perhaps he'll believe me."

"Well, I'm certainly impressed, I don't mind admitting that. Mind you—"

"There's Denny!" Nicola interrupted, leaping forward. He hadn't gone off without her after all. He was waiting on the corner of the road, by the National Westminster Bank. She might have known he wouldn't really have gone home without saying something.

"Been here for ages," he said as she ran up to him. "I began to think you weren't ever gonna come."

"So why didn't you *wait?*"

"I did wait, I told you. Been waiting for ages!"

"No, but at school!"

Denny made a face. She looked at him, frowning. "What's that s'posed to mean?"

"You were behaving like Rose," said Denny.

"I was not!" She was outraged. How could anyone *ever* accuse her of behaving like Rose? Rose, who screamed and ran around shrieking? Nicola had never run around like that in her life. "I wasn't behaving a *bit* like Rose!"

"Yes, you were . . . just like her."

Denny always stuck doggedly to any point that he had made. That was because he didn't usually make one without first having given it serious consideration. Had she *really* been behaving like Rose?

She heard herself screaming across a crowd of people at Cheryl, saw herself simpering at Mr. French, basking in the approval of Mr. Henry, listening enraptured as people told her how wonderful she was.

"You were enjoying it," said Denny.

He sounded accusing. Nicola felt suddenly cross.

"Why shouldn't I enjoy it?" It was nice to be told that you were talented. Anyone would enjoy it—even Denny.

They stomped along for a while in silence. From some way behind came her mother's voice, "You be sure you stick to the main road! I don't want you going over by that park."

It was embarrassing, having parents trail you only a few hundred feet behind. You couldn't hold hands with parents that close by. In a small voice, Nicola said, "Didn't you like it?"

"Yeah, I thought it was great."

"But didn't you like *me*?"

"Course I did," said Denny.

"So why didn't you *say* something?"

"Didn't need me telling you," said Denny. "Not with everybody else doing it."

CHAPTER ✣ *Seven*

On the Monday after the school performance, Nicola's report card arrived in its familiar brown envelope. It came while the family was still at breakfast, which was rather embarrassing because Mr. Bruce slit open the envelope then and there (the first time he had ever done such a thing) and, having skimmed through the contents, he proceeded to read them out so that everyone could hear.

"*English:* Nicola has worked extremely well this term. *French:* She shows a good grasp of the language. *Computer Studies:* She has taken an intelligent interest. *Math:* Nicola is not a mathematician but has achieved a respectable average through sheer determination and hard work. *Physical Education:* A naturally gifted athlete. *Music:* She applies herself well and has a good ear. *Biology:* An excellent half-term's work. Nicola should go far in this subject. *Needlework—*"

Needlework wasn't very good. Mrs. Hibbert com-

plained that she didn't take the subject seriously and
made "'scant effort to overcome natural deficiencies."
Rose, sarcastically, said, "Glad to know she's *got* some
natural deficiencies." Nicola didn't blame her. If anyone had read out a report like that on Rose, she would
have felt like vomiting all across the table. Of course
she was happy to hear nice things said about herself,
but after Denny's accusations on Saturday she was
being especially careful not to show it. She just
turned a bit pink and mushed her oatmeal around
with a spoon and made a few mumbling noises.

"S'pose you think you're too clever for needlework," said Rose.

"If she did, it would be very silly." Mrs. Bruce
spoke briskly, nodding at Nicola over the teapot as
she did so. "It's never clever to be impractical."

"I'm not impractical," said Nicola. She might not
be able to sew in a straight line or do a lazy daisy
stitch to save her life, but she could make things out of
pieces of wood and she could put model kits together
and she could work with a small handsaw. She could
even mend fuses and knew how to change washers on
water taps, which was more than Rose could do.

"You'll find a knowledge of needlework comes in
very handy," said Mrs. Bruce. "You won't always
have dressers running around after you ready to take
up hems and put tucks in things."

"Not unless you get to be a star," said Rose.

"What about this biology, then?" Mr. Bruce tapped
a finger against the report.

"What about it?" said Mrs. Bruce.

"Isn't this comment by the woman who also teaches
physics and what have you later on?"

"She teaches the ninth-graders," said Nicola. "Miss Khan teaches you after that."

"Who's Miss Khan?" Rose wanted to know.

"She was new last term. It used to be Mr. Gorringe, but he was horrible. Now it's Miss Khan."

Nicola had been looking forward to reaching tenth grade and studying physics and chemistry with Miss Khan. She'd been looking forward to ninth grade and studying further with Miss Richardson as well. She reminded herself, just in time, that in all probability she still *would* be doing it. It wasn't in the least likely that she would be accepted by Kendra Hall.

"Ninety-nine percent," said Mr. Bruce. "That's a pretty good mark."

"She always gets that in biology. It's a pity she can't work as hard at things like needlework and home economics. Those rolls she brought home last year were like lead pellets."

Rose giggled and said, "D'you remember that time she put the sugar in the oven to dry, and it all went and melted?"

"Yes, I do," said Mrs. Bruce. "I also remember the time she scrubbed a polished table for me with bleach."

"That was when I was *five!*" said Nicola.

"Yes. Well, in some respects I'd say you haven't changed much. Anyone who can deliberately cut holes in a perfectly good carpet—"

"I didn't *deliberately.*"

The carpet was a sore point. It was Nicola's old bedroom carpet, and it wasn't as good as all that. It had worn patches in the middle and was starting to fray at the edges. It was the fraying that had caused all the trouble because the frayed bits kept catching in the glass-fronted doors of her bookcase. (The bookcase was Victorian, and she had inherited it from a great aunt.) Cutting away a tiny piece of carpet had seemed at the time the obvious solution. She saw now that it wasn't, but she hadn't seen it that way *then*, so what she did could hardly be called deliberate. And anyway that had been almost three months ago. You'd have thought it would have been forgotten by now.

"Who's this Miss Camfield?" said Mr. Bruce.

"She's my homeroom teacher and gym teacher."

"According to her, Nicola is a sensible and responsible girl who is an asset to the school community."

Rose made a cackling sound like a goose. Mrs. Bruce said, "Sensible! She obviously doesn't know what she's like with carpets. Nicola, why are you messing around with that oatmeal?"

"I don't *like* oatmeal." It was horrible, nasty, chewy stuff.

"You just eat it. It's good for you."

"It's awful. I don't want it." She pushed her plate away. "I've got to go out anyhow. I'm meeting Denny."

"Why?" said Mrs. Bruce. "Where are you going?"

"We're going up to the Arena on Earl Street. There's a computer show."

"Well, make sure you're back in plenty of time to rest. You've got a dance class at five, don't forget."

She hardly could. She was having classes every day now until the audition.

"You be back no later than three. It's tiring, traipsing around at those shows. You really ought to be staying at home, taking things easy for the next few days. In fact—"

Nicola fled. She had promised Denny weeks ago that she would go to the computer show with him. She wasn't backing out now, audition or no audition.

The great day arrived. Denny, the night before, had somewhat bashfully wished her good luck. "Hope you get in, if that's what you want." Rose, in her best theatrical tradition, had sent her a card; her father, as he left for work, said, "Well! So this is it, then? The Day of Reckoning."

The audition was at eleven o'clock, so there was no time to waste. Before going to bed the previous night, Nicola had packed a bag containing everything she would need—one pair of soft shoes, one pair of pointe shoes, leotard, tights, leg warmers in case it was cold, sweater likewise, a band for her hair, a supply of hair clips. After she had packed it all, Mrs. Bruce had come in and unpacked it again, just to check, "Because you know you can't be trusted," but there hadn't been anything missing. Nicola wasn't anywhere near as careless as her mother liked to make out—not when it came to things that mattered.

Mrs. French wasn't able to accompany her to the audition because she was pregnant and had to stay in bed a lot of the time. Apparently people didn't always have to stay in bed when they were pregnant—just sometimes, if the baby was misbehaving or threatening to arrive too early, which was what Mrs. French's baby was doing.

"I told you," said Rose, "it's *dreadful,* being pregnant . . . I'm not going to, *ever.*"

Nicola didn't think it was dreadful, exactly, but agreed it was certainly a nuisance. It meant that instead of traveling across town with Mrs. French, feeling pleasantly mature and sophisticated, she had to go with her mother and be reduced to the status of a mere child, and be told "not to sit and frown" and to "remember to go to the toilet on the train because we don't want to have to do it at Victoria Station." Nicola didn't like going to the toilet on trains. Everyone knew where you were going and what you were going there for. She had just decided that she would hold herself until she reached Kendra Hall, even if she did feel as if she were bursting, when her mother said, "We're almost at Victoria Station. You'd better go. You know what you're like."

"It's all right," said Nicola. "I can wait."

"That's what you say now. We've still got a long subway ride ahead of us. You just do as you're told and go."

She knew that if she didn't there would only be an embarrassing scene. Head held high and cheeks flaring, she marched out of the compartment. She was glad, afterward, because the subway ride *was* long (thirteen stops on the district line, all the way out to a place called Ealing), but it still didn't soothe her fierce resentment at being treated like a *child*.

They reached Kendra Hall at half past ten. It was just as Mrs. French had described it—just as it looked from the photographs in the brochure. It had once been somebody's manor house and was full of oak paneling and funny creaky staircases with balconies running around the top of a central hall. Nicola thought it must be wonderful to live in a house as old as that. All Mrs. Bruce said was, "You'd never keep the dust down." Imagine worrying about a little thing like *dust* here.

There were eleven other girls besides Nicola taking the audition. Some shrieked a lot and showed off, like Rose, talking to one another in loud voices as they changed. Others, like Nicola, stayed very quiet and just got on with the business of smoothing the wrinkles out of their tights and securing their hair with clasps. Nicola wondered if deep down the ones who shrieked were as nervous as the ones who didn't shriek, or whether there really were people who could attend an audition for a place like Kendra Hall and not feel anything. She herself wasn't actually *paralyzed*. Mrs. French had told her, "Take it in your stride. It'll be no different from any ordinary class." But she couldn't suppress an odd jittery feeling now and then.

The first jittery feeling occurred when they were called into the studio and found no less than four people waiting for them. One, who was quite young and prettyish, was introduced as Miss Flowerdew. She was the one who was to give the class. The other three—a severe-looking, elderly lady with gold-rimmed spectacles; a very plump, smiling lady in a white coat; and a small, spidery man with little dark eyes that darted continually this way and that—sat in a row, like the Inquisition, on hard, high-backed chairs behind a table. Nicola could see that they all had notebooks in front of them and pens, ready for making notes. She tried to imagine what they would write about her—*Nicola Bruce: Weak allegro? Poor elevation? Clumsy footwork?* Except that she wouldn't

be Nicola Bruce. She would be number fourteen because that was what she had been given to pin to her
chest.

The class, as Mrs. French had promised, was very
much the same as an ordinary class, though try as you
might you could never *quite* forget that this was an
audition and that Kendra Hall was one of the best
ballet schools in the country. Nor could you forget
that there were three people sitting behind a table, all
taking notes and watching you like hawks.

When they came to *adagio*, which Nicola had been
looking forward to, she was a bit disappointed. The
steps they were given seemed so simple—*chassé, attitudes croisées, en face, effacées;* then *arabesque fon-
due allongée, pas de bourrée dessus.* They might
almost, she thought, have been back in their first year
of ballet. And then they came to *allegro,* and that was
when she had her second really bad moment of the jit-
ters because the *allegro* was so fearsomely and hideously complex that she just knew she was never
going to get through it. She only had time to think
how *unfair* it was before the music had started and
they were off. *Sauté, changement, glissade derrière ...*

She made it until about three quarters of the way
through, when quite suddenly the girl who was num-
bered fifteen, and who should by rights have been
turning diagonally away from Nicola, turned diagonally toward her instead, so that for one split-second
their astonished glances met. Rose wouldn't have been
thrown off by this because Rose never was. Even
when Rose was wrong (which she had been known to
be), she continued regardless. Nicola hesitated for
just that split-second and was lost. She picked up

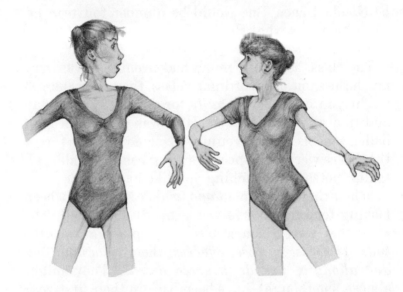

again, but her concentration had gone. She didn't exactly disgrace herself, but she could hardly believe
that she had come up to the high standards of Kendra
Hall. The only consolation was that several other people besides number fifteen had become hopelessly
muddled. Nicola hadn't actually become muddled but
had only fluffed it a little. Still there were probably
some people who hadn't fluffed it at all.

As they left the studio, the girl marked fifteen said,
"That was *aw*ful. I thought I was going to *die*. I'm so
sorry."

"That's all right," said Nicola. "Not your fault."

The half hour that followed was decidedly nerve-
wracking. They all had to wrap up warm and join
their chaperones (mostly other mothers) in something called the Green Room, which was a sort of
lounge, for milk and cookies while they waited to hear

who had been called back to be interviewed by Miss
Gover, the principal, and who was going to be politely
told, "You may go now."

Most people, including Nicola, drank their milk
and nibbled their cookies in a ghostly kind of silence.
Only numbers sixteen and twenty-one, evidently
bolder than the rest, continued to jabber and shriek,
and even they didn't jabber quite so fiercely or shriek
quite so loudly as they had before. The mothers, however, more than made up for it. If they had been at
school, thought Nicola, they would all have been sent
to stand in the corner and collect bad conduct marks a
long time ago.

She heard Mrs. Bruce say, "Of course, Nicola takes
classes from Pamela French. I suppose in a way that
gives her an advantage. It means she's already familiar with the Kendra Hall style. But then I don't imagine Mrs. French would have taken her on if she hadn't
thought she was the right material. She doesn't take
just anyone; she's very particular. She doesn't normally accept pupils until they've reached a fairly advanced stage. Of course, she took Nicola when she was
only eleven. She actually asked me for her."

Nicola cringed. Her only consolation was that all
the other mothers were doing it as well.

At the end of thirty minutes Miss Flowerdew came
back into the room and smiled and said she would like
numbers fourteen, fifteen, nineteen, and twenty-one
to step outside, with their chaperones. General appre-
hension. Did that mean, thank you, you may go—or
did it mean, you are being called for an interview?

In the same ghostly silence numbers fourteen, fifteen, nineteen, and twenty-one made their way from

the room, followed by four grim-faced mothers carrying coats and sweaters and handbags full of glucose
tablets and vitamin pills.

"All right," said Miss Flowerdew, "if you'd care to
come this way, Miss Gover would like to speak to you
all individually."

The four mothers exchanged glances of triumph.
Number twenty-one, who was bold, gave a big, happy
grin. The others just gulped and swallowed and grew
a bit pink (or in Nicola's case white, since she always
turned white when she was anxious).

Miss Gover was the severe-looking, elderly lady
with gold-rimmed spectacles who had been at the audition. She was with the little, spidery man, whom she
introduced as Mr. Bregonzi. (His name was in the
brochure at the head of the list of teaching staff. He
mainly taught the senior boys and advanced *pas de
deux.*) To Nicola's relief, Mrs. Bruce had been asked
if she would mind waiting outside. She didn't like
having to talk to people in front of her mother. It
made it impossible, sometimes, to say what you really
wanted to say. But by herself she didn't mind talking
to anybody.

Miss Gover asked most of the questions—all about
how long she had been studying ballet and what made
her think she wanted to be a dancer and was she prepared for all the hard work and dedication involved?
To the last question Nicola said yes, she was, because
she had had to drop out of the under-fifteen hockey
team just a few days ago *and* hadn't been able to go
swimming or play table tennis because of all the extra
classes she was having. Mr. Bregonzi said, "And how
do you feel about that? Do you resent it?"

"Sometimes," said Nicola.

"Do you ever find yourself wishing that you could be just an ordinary schoolgirl and *not* study ballet?"

"Mmm . . . " She wrinkled her nose, considering. "I think I *am* quite ordinary, actually, but sometimes I wish that you could study ballet without having to stop doing other things."

"That," said Miss Gover, "would be having your cake and eating it, too."

"Yes, I know," said Nicola.

"And that as you must realize, is not possible."

"No," said Nicola.

"So, then—" Miss Gover removed her spectacles. Her eyes, without them, looked pale and staring, like the eyes of a fish. "Are there any questions that you would like to ask us? Anything about the school, about the classes?"

Nicola thought a while. Then shyly she said, "I'd like to know if I could still take physics and chemistry."

"Physics and chemistry?" Miss Gover turned to look at Mr. Bregonzi. "That's a strange one! We've never had that question before."

Mr. Bregonzi leaned forward.

"Why do you want to know?"

"Well, because if I stayed on at school, I could do it, and I just thought it'd be nice if I could still do it if I came to Kendra Hall—I mean, if I were accepted. But maybe . . . " (maybe she shouldn't have said anything about it in the first place) ". . . maybe it's another cake thing, like not being able to play hockey."

"Yes, I'm afraid it is," said Miss Gover. "We simply don't have room in the curriculum to cover the full range of academic courses. I wish we did, but there just aren't enough hours in the day. You'll find you have your work cut out as it is. If of course"—she re-settled her spectacles on her nose—"we are able to offer you a place. I hope that we shall be, but you do realize we have literally hundreds of applicants every year and only a very few vacancies? Particularly in your age group. Anyway"—she smiled, a rather frost-nipped smile, but still a smile—"one way or another you'll be hearing from us within the next week or two. So until then—"

"Just contain yourself and be patient," Mr. Bre-gonzi said, also smiling. It was a friendlier smile than Miss Gover's. "I know that's easier said than done, but . . . do your best!"

After the interview came the medical examination with the very plump lady in the white coat who was a doctor. She laughed a lot and said she thought she could safely promise that Nicola would never grow as big as she was *width*-wise, but lengthwise was another matter. By the time she reached her full height, she might very possibly be pushing the limit, which for girls was 5'7".

"Not that there aren't dancers who are taller than that, so if you do start shooting up there's no need to fall into despair. It's just that they really prefer to have Miss Average for the *corps de ballet*. It ruins their pretty patterns if they have one lanky beanpole amid a neat little forest of garden flowers."

It had always been one of her mother's greatest dreads that Nicola would turn into a lanky beanpole. She fretted about it all the way home.

"It would really be too bad if they turned you down

just for that. I still can't think where you get it from. *I'm* not tall; your father's not tall. Tell me again what Miss Gover said to you."

She had already told her mother what Miss Gover had said to her. Dutifully she repeated it.

"She said she hoped they'd be able to offer me a place, but they had hundreds of applicants and I'd be hearing from them in a week or two."

"And what happened before that? What sorts of questions did she ask you?"

"Mmm . . . she asked me if I minded not being able to play hockey and things."

"And what did you say?"

"I said sometimes I did, but—"

"You shouldn't have said that!" Mrs. Bruce sounded agitated. "She was obviously trying to find out how much ballet means to you! What on earth made you go and say a thing like that for?"

"Well, it's true," said Nicola. "I *do* sometimes resent it."

"*Resent* it?" Now her mother sounded even more agitated. "I hope you didn't use that word to Miss Gover?"

"*They* used it. Then Mr. Bregonzi asked me if I ever wished I could be just an ordinary schoolgirl, and I said I thought I *was* quite ordinary, but—"

"But what?"

"Well, I just said there were *some* times when I wished you could study ballet and not have to give up other things. Like yesterday, when Cheryl and Sarah came over and you wouldn't let me go out on my bike because you said I'd be sure to do something stupid like falling off and bruising myself and not be fit for the audition. I just wished I could go out on my bike *and* do the audition."

Her mother looked at her anxiously.

"You didn't tell them that?"

"Yes." Why shouldn't she have told them? "They asked me. They wanted to know. They were *interested.* They wouldn't have asked if they weren't, would they?"

Mrs. Bruce shook her head.

"Honestly, Nicola," she said, "there are times when I simply despair of you."

CHAPTER ❧ *Eight*

"Contain yourself and be patient," Mr. Bregonzi had said. Nicola tried her best, but as even Mr. Bregonzi had admitted, containing yourself and being patient was easier said than done. She went for bicycle rides with Cheryl and Sarah, spent hours drinking milk shakes in the Treat Shop, played table tennis and went swimming with Denny, did all the things that she hadn't been able to do before the audition. Every morning she went flying downstairs to look at the mail, and every time the telephone rang she waited breathlessly, hanging over the banisters or with one ear pressed to a crack in the door, as her mother answered it. After all, they hadn't said *how* she would hear from them, only that she would do so in a week or two. They might just as easily telephone as write a letter.

The week or two came and went. The day that school began again after the spring break was the day on which she should have heard. As she arrived at school, Linda Baker came bustling up.

"Well?" she said, all bossy and dictatorial. "What happened? Did you get in?"

"Don't know yet," said Nicola. "Haven't heard."

"Haven't *heard?* After all this time?"

"That's a bad sign," said Janice Martin. "If they're going to offer you a place, they usually do it right away."

"They said a week or two," said Nicola.

"That's what they *say.* "

"When my brother applied for college," said Sarah, "he didn't hear for weeks and *weeks.* And then they suddenly wrote and said he'd gotten in."

"That's college," Linda Baker spoke witheringly. "It's not the same as ballet school."

Just before morning roll call, Denny came up to her.

"Did you hear yet?"

She shook her head.

"Prob'ly come in the next mail," said Denny. "My mom was expecting something this morning, and that didn't come either."

She was grateful to Denny for trying to cheer her up, but she had a nagging suspicion that Janice Martin might be right. If they had decided to offer her a place, they would surely have done so by now? Miss Gover had warned her that they had only a few vacancies, and then there was the possibility that she might grow too tall, and probably she *shouldn't* have said that bit about sometimes feeling resentful, even if it had been true.

The first homeroom period after the spring break was always devoted to general discussion and the election of class monitors for the next half-term. Sarah put Nicola's name forward for girls' softball captain, and Miss Camfield looked inquiringly at her.

"Will that be all right, Nicola? I take it you'll be able to play?"

She remembered what Denny had said. It was like being an *invalid* . . . Linda Baker, who had also been nominated for girls' softball captain, waved a hand.

"She hasn't heard yet whether she's gotten in or not."

"No—well, these things take time. In the meantime—" Miss Camfield turned and under "Linda Baker" wrote "Nicola Bruce." "Anyone else?"

One of the boys, who shouldn't have had anything to do with it since the boys didn't play the girls' slow-pitch softball, said, "Michelle Brown," and everyone jeered—not so much because Michelle Brown was easily the world's worst softball player, but because everyone knew that she and Alan Argent had a thing going. Nicola was glad that she and Denny didn't embarrass each other like that.

Voting took place by a show of hands, with Nicola being elected captain and Linda Baker as assistant captain. Linda Baker wasn't terribly pleased because last year it had been the other way around, but lots of people had complained about her bossiness and how rude she was, and had threatened to quit. Sarah, leaning backward in her chair, whispered, "Hope you get into ballet school, but I hope you don't have to resign from being captain 'cause if you do, I'm not playing under *her* again."

After all the monitors and team captains had been elected, Miss Camfield said they really ought to spend a bit of time discussing future plans, because this was the time of year when they had to decide which study program they wanted to enter next year: Languages, Science, or General Studies. Denny was going into the Science program; he had known ever since elementary school that he wanted to work with computers. Sarah was going to take Languages, and Cheryl had decided on General Studies, which meant that for the first time the three of them—Sarah, Cheryl, and Nicola—were going to be split up. They had talked about it quite often, trying to find a solution, but there just didn't seem to be one. Sarah was hopeless at anything scientific, Cheryl was only good at needlework (she had already make Nicola promise that when she was famous, she would let Cheryl design her dresses for her), and no one had any doubts but that Nicola would go on to the Science program.

"Let's start at the back," said Miss Camfield. "Alan, what ideas have you got?"

A voice Nicola recognized as belonging to Mark Humphries said, "Get Michelle Brown behind a bush," and most of the boys and quite a few of the girls laughed. Nicola couldn't see whether Denny did or not. She hoped that he didn't, but as Mrs. Bruce always said, tight-lipped, "Boys are like that."

"You can cut out the smart talk," said Miss Camfield, uncertain who had spoken. "We've got a lot to get through. We don't have time for that sort of thing. All right, Alan?"

Alan Argent was one of those people without a thought in his head. Nicola didn't know why Miss Camfield wasted her breath trying to communicate with him. Some of the others weren't much better.

Some, on the other hand, like Denny and Sarah (who wanted to work in a travel agency so she could get free flights to places like America and Russia), had lots of thoughts and were only too willing to express them. Nicola would have been willing to express hers if Miss Camfield had asked her. She was quite ready to explain how if she didn't get into ballet school, then she was going to apply for college and study to become a doctor. But to her disappointment Miss Camfield didn't bother. All she said when she reached Nicola was "Nicola, you're waiting for the result of your audition, of course. Cheryl, how abut you?" and they all had to listen to Cheryl rambling on about her needlework.

On the way home that afternoon across the park (only now they went by a different route, one which couldn't be seen from the windows of buses), Denny said, "What're you all jittery for?"

"I'm not all jittery," said Nicola, but now that he had mentioned it, she knew that he was right. She *was* all jittery. She had been jittery all day long.

"Is it on account of not hearing?"

"S'pose so."

Up until now she had just about been able to contain herself. Today, because this was the day when the two weeks were up, she had hardly been able to think of anything else. She had listened while the others babbled on and on about school events, and for the first time it had all seemed so terribly small and unimportant. The only thing that mattered was the result of her audition.

"What'll you do," said Denny, "if you don't get in?"

Go away and howl, all by herself, she thought. She had already made plans for it. She was going to take Ben, and they were going to go off together on a long, long walk, just the two of them, not even with Denny, until she felt strong enough to face the world again. The last thing she would be able to bear would be to stay indoors and hear Rose saying how sorry she was and telling her how Susie Siegenberg's sister hadn't gotten in either, and her mother alternately grumbling at her for having ruined her chances and bewailing the fact that it was because she was too tall. "I *still* don't know where you get it from." When Nicola was upset, she liked to be alone.

"Would you try for somewhere else?" said Denny.

"Not sure. Don't think so."

"Why not? You would if it was college. You wouldn't just try one place and then give up."

"N-no, but—" This was different. If she failed Kendra Hall, she didn't really think that she would want to go anywhere else. Maybe the Royal Ballet School, but even that wouldn't be the same. Kendra Hall was where Mrs. French had gone and where she wanted Nicola to go.

"Seems to me," said Denny, "you can't want to do it as badly as all that."

She wanted to get into *Kendra Hall* as badly as all that. She wanted to get into Kendra Hall more than anything else in the world. Denny couldn't understand. There was no point in trying to explain to him. To people who weren't dancers, one ballet school probably seemed very much the same as any other.

"Let's not talk about it." Deliberately, trying to make believe she didn't care, she gave a little twirl—

and then stopped. Giving little twirls in public places was behaving like Rose. Furthermore it embarrassed people. She fell back a pace and slipped her hand into Denny's. "Did you laugh, this morning, when Mark Humphries made that joke?"

"What joke?"

"About Alan Argent wanting to take Michelle Brown behind a bush."

"Didn't hear it," said Denny.

"Would you have if you had heard it?"

"Prob'ly." Denny grinned. "Girls like Michelle Brown, not much else you can do with 'em."

"Don't be *pig*like." Nicola swung her book bag, catching him with a hearty smack on the arm. Sometimes she didn't wonder at her mother for not liking boys. If even Denny were "like that," then what hope was there for the rest of them?

The first thing Nicola did on arriving home was to say hello to Ben. It was the first thing that anyone did. There was simply no escaping it. The second thing she did was catch a quick glance at the kitchen table.

Nothing. Her heart dropped like a chunk of stone, clank-thump, down into her shoes. Whenever there were letters for either Rose or Nicola, Mrs. Bruce always put them by the side of their plates, ready for opening. Not that there usually *was* anything for Nicola, except on those occasions when she had written away for catalogs or free samples. There was quite often something for Rose because children who had seen her on television wrote her fan letters asking for photographs or wanting to know how they could get on television and do the things that she did. Today

there was nothing by either of their plates. Come to
think of it, there weren't any *plates*, either. Nicola
stared. Where was her snack? Where was Mrs. Bruce?

"Hey!" The door suddenly crashed open, and Rose
burst in. She grabbed Nicola by the arm. "I've got
something to show you!"

"What?"

"Never mind what!" Rose tugged at her, impatient.
"Come and see!"

"Why?" She wasn't in a mood for being tugged at.
She wanted her snack. She wanted bread and jam
with lots of butter, and huge, squishy cakes oozing
cream filling that would make her loathsomely and
disgustingly fat.

"Just stop asking *questions,"* said Rose.

Disgruntled, Nicola allowed herself to be dragged
out of the kitchen, up the hall, and into the living
room.

"Look."

She looked. The table was laid out as if for a birthday party. There were candies and nuts in little card-
board plates, and chocolate ice cream, colored paper
napkins, fruit salad, and a container of real whipped
cream. And right in the middle, a pink-iced cake in
the shape of a ballet shoe.

Nicola turned, wonderingly, first to Rose and then
to her mother.

"You *see?"* said Rose.

Mrs. Bruce was on the telephone, talking excitedly.
As Nicola came in, she said, "Here she is now, Mother.
You can tell her yourself. Nicola!" She flapped a
hand. "Come and talk to your grandmother."

With one last bewildered glance at the pink-iced

cake, Nicola took the receiver that her mother was holding out.

"Gran?"

"Who's a clever girl, then? Now we've *two* grand-daughters we can boast about! You wait till your granddad gets to hear of it. He's out at the moment, but the minute he comes back—"

Nicola turned, once again, to look at the table and its array of goodies. She saw now what she hadn't seen before. By the side of one of the plates there was an envelope. Mrs. Bruce picked it up and waved it at her, nodding triumphantly as she did so.

Gran's voice was still speaking to her out of the telephone.

"So how do you feel? Do you feel excited? I do, and I know your mother does! Anyway, my dear, I'll let you go and have your party because I'm sure you're having something special, and I expect your grand-father will call you later. How about that?"

"Yes," said Nicola. She felt in a daze. She felt as if she were living in *Alice in Wonderland,* and it was all going to turn into a dream. Numbly she replaced the receiver.

"Here you are!" Mrs. Bruce held out the envelope. "It's yours. Take it!"

Nicola did so. She held it a moment, examining it and turning it over in her hands, studying the stamp and the postmark. The envelope had already been opened. It was untidily ripped, which was the way Mrs. Bruce always opened letters. Nicola, perhaps because she received so few of them, liked to do the job neatly and carefully, taking her time, slitting the top with a paper knife or ruler so that when she had removed the letter and read it, she could fold it back up and put it away again.

"Aren't you going to look?" cried Rose shrilly.

Dutifully she removed the sheet of paper from the ruined envelope. It was addressed to her, quite plainly, on the front, in typed letters: *Ms. Nicola Bruce, 10 Fenning Road, Streatham, London S.W. 16.* Rose and her mother were watching her with a kind of eager anticipation.

"Well?" said Mrs. Bruce.

Reluctantly Nicola opened the letter and unfolded it. It wasn't the same, reading a letter that had already been read by someone else. It said:

> *Dear Nicola,*
>
> *We are pleased to tell you that we are able to offer you a place at Kendra Hall starting in September of this year.*
>
> *We hope that you will be able to accept it and that we shall see you here next term.*
>
> *We shall be writing to your parents in a day or two with details.*
>
> *Yours sincerely,*
> *Barbara Flowerdew*
> *Head of Ballet Studies*
> *Junior School*

"*Well?*" Rose was almost dancing on the spot. "Aren't you going to say anything?"

"It came by special delivery," said Mrs. Bruce. "I thought I'd better open it, just in case it was bad news."

"Honestly," said Rose, "hardly *any*body gets into

Kendra Hall. Susie Siegenberg's going to be absolutely *green*."

"I'd already made the cake," said Mrs. Bruce, "some time ago. If you hadn't gotten in, I was going to keep it for your birthday."

"Look," said Rose, "it's even got *ribbons.*"

Sure enough, there were two beautiful pink satin ribbons attached, just where the ribbons on a real ballet shoe would be. They trailed artistically across the table, threading among the candies, nuts, ice cream, and cake.

"I'd have sent you a telegram," said Rose, "if there'd been time."

"Gran and Grandpa Bruce up north will send a telegram. I called them immediately after I opened the letter. They're as pleased as can be. They said to give you their congratulations. Oh, and I told Mrs. French. I knew you'd want her to know. She's on cloud nine. She said she'll see you tomorrow when you've had time to get over the excitement. There's no point in having a class this evening. You'd never be able to concentrate. We both agreed that a bit of a celebration is in order."

"Wait till you tell Janice Martin," said Rose. Rose knew all about Janice Martin, having been at Madam Paula's with her. "I bet she'll be even greener than Susie Siegenberg."

"I told Mrs. Kemp up the road. She said she could hardly believe it. Nicola's always been such a *gawky* child." Mrs. Bruce laughed happily. "I said we hadn't been able to believe it, at first. I still remember that day Mrs. French asked me if you could go and take lessons with her. *Nicola?* I said. How could anyone want *Nicola?* Well, she's proved us all wrong!"

"*I* knew," said Rose. "That time I let her stand in for me in the mime show."

Rose hadn't let her stand in for her. Mr. Marlowe, who had been the producer, had wanted Nicola in Rose's place, and Rose had sulked and screamed for a week until Nicola had stood down again. She knelt and put her arms around Ben's neck.

"Aren't you thrilled?" said Rose.

"Course I am," said Nicola quietly.

"You don't *sound* like it. I'd be turning cartwheels!"

"Go and wash your hands," said Mrs. Bruce. "Let's have our party."

Nicola rubbed her cheek against Ben's.

"What did Dad say?"

"Oh, I haven't told your father! You know what he's like—no interest in anything outside soccer and his gardening. You can tell him when he comes in."

She wished she could have told Mrs. French. She could still tell Denny, of course, and Cheryl and Sarah—*and* Janice Martin. She would really enjoy telling Janice Martin, but Mrs. French was the one she had really been looking forward to telling. She had even gone so far, once or twice, as to allow herself the luxury of imagining how it would be running up the road, banging with the big lion's head knocker on Mrs. French's front door, Mrs. French coming to open it . . .

"Hello, Nicola! What brings you here at this time of the day?"

"I've just had a letter from Kendra Hall."

"*Oh?*"

A moment of anxiety, while Nicola would savor the fact that she knew and Mrs. French didn't. Then, "Here! You can read it!"

But now Mrs. French had already been told.

"I wish you'd go and *wash,*" said Rose. "We can't start eating till you're ready."

Slowly Nicola got to her feet.

"Shouldn't we wait till Dad gets in?"

"I'm not waiting till then! I'm *starving!*"

"We'll save him a piece of cake," said Mrs. Bruce. "You go and scrub those dirty hands while I put the kettle on."

Obediently Nicola went across to the door.

"What did Mrs. French say when you told her?"

"She said that's absolutely wonderful, I always knew Nicola had it in her—which she did, of course. One has to hand it to her. The rest of us didn't see it, but she did."

"*I* did," said Rose.

Rose was such a liar. Nobody had seen it except for Mrs. French. Nicola closed the door behind her and trailed up the stairs, Ben bounding along at her side. Once in the bathroom she turned both taps full on so that the water swirled and rushed around the bowl, spraying drops all over. Ben, excited, stood and barked.

She didn't care if the carpet did get wet. It was stupid having a carpet in a bathroom.

She didn't care if the neighbors complained about Ben barking. Dogs ought to be allowed to bark. It was their way of expressing themselves.

She plunged both hands into the gushing water, creating tidal waves. Slop, slurp onto the floor.

"When will you ever learn, Nicola? That carpet will rot if you keep getting it wet."

That had been *her* letter, addressed to *her*.

People shouldn't open other people's letters. They had no right.

"I thought I'd better, just in case it was bad news . . ."

But it hadn't been bad news. It had been glorious, marvelous, incredibly fantastic news, and this ought to be the most glorious, marvelous, incredibly fantastic moment of her whole life.

She wondered why it was that she suddenly felt like *crying.*

CHAPTER ✤ *Nine*

"Nicola Tulip."

"Nicola *Rose.*"

Giggle, giggle. Great hilarity.

"Nicola Daffodil."

"Nicola Geranium."

"Nicola *Mimosa!*"

Tee-hee. Ho-ho. Ha-ha.

"I've told you," said Nicola. "I'm staying as I am."
She might just as well not have bothered saying it.
Nobody took the slightest bit of notice. Cheryl, scrambling onto her desk top, raised an imaginary trumpet
to her lips.

"Ta-ra-ta-ra! Introducing, in the far corner . . . Nicola . . . Mimosa!"

"Nicolette de la Mimose."

"De la Bruce."

"Brucel*los*is!"

"That's a disease," said Nicola. "It's what cows
get."

Janice Martin snickered, whether at the display of ignorance or because she thought it funny that Nicola might call herself after a disease there was no way of knowing. Mr. Kenny came into the room at that point to give a geography lesson, and all conversation had to cease. It didn't stop Janice Martin from passing her a note that read *How about Nicola Bindweed?* Extraordinarily childish sense of humor some people had.

"Would you really want to be famous?" Denny said to her later, as they walked home. She thought about it.

"Wouldn't mind."

"I wouldn't," said Denny.

"Wouldn't you?"

He shook his head, very definite.

"I wouldn't mind inventing something and being written about in magazines and things, but I wouldn't want to be famous like a TV star and have everyone keep on recognizing me all the time."

"Mmm. I s'pose it might get to be a bit of a nuisance."

"Dead boring," said Denny.

"But it would be nice to think that everyone had heard of you."

"Don't see why."

Upon reflection, Nicola wasn't sure that she could see why, either. After all, what difference would it make?

"You'd get letters," she said, hopefully. "That'd be nice—hundreds and hundreds each day. I'd like that."

"Bet you wouldn't if you had to answer 'em all."

"I'd have a secretary. She'd do all the answering. I'd only have to read them."

Denny grunted, plainly not convinced. Nicola thought about it a bit more.

"Perhaps I wouldn't actually want to be *world*-famous—just a *little* bit famous, so I'd get just a *few* letters, and just *some*times people'd stop me in the street and say things to me."

On that basis, though, she already was "just a little bit famous." No fewer than three people from Fenning Road had stopped her on the way to school that morning to congratulate her. First there had been Mrs. Hope, the lady next door, who had been putting out her milk bottles just as Nicola was leaving. Then there had been Mr. Kemp, who was the husband of Mrs. Kemp, who had "hardly been able to believe it" (*Nicola was always such a gawky child* ...). Mr. Kemp had been getting into his car and had gotten out of it again to say, "Splendid piece of news! Well done!" The third person had been crotchety Miss Dunk from number fifteen, whom Rose always referred to as "the old bag across the road." Practically the only times Miss Dunk had ever spoken to Nicola were to tell her off for letting Ben cock his leg against her picket fence or for rattling sticks against the fence or kicking tin cans in the gutter. This morning she had beckoned with a finger, and when Nicola reluctantly had crossed over (what had she done wrong *now?*), Miss Dunk beamed at her and said, "Well! I understand we have a little Anna Pavlova in our midst?" It was a rather yucky sort of thing to say, but at least it was better than being lectured for bad manners or for noisiness.

"S'pose you think you're quite famous already," said Denny.

She felt her cheeks grow hot.

"Course I don't!"

"Way everyone was carrying on before school this morning, anyone'd think you'd been made Queen of England."

"Well, that's not my fault!"

Denny said "Humph!" and hunched a shoulder. She looked at him crossly.

"Why are you being so mean?" she said.

Denny kicked a stone.

"Not being mean."

"You are! You're being monstrous!"

If it had been Linda Baker or Janice Martin, she would have put it down as ordinary jealousy, but Denny wasn't like that. He hadn't been jealous a year ago, when she'd won the seventh-grade class prize for Hard Work and Endeavor, any more than she'd been jealous when he'd ranked first in the under-fourteen section of the Computer Club competition organized by the Junior Chamber of Commerce. He certainly wouldn't be jealous of her getting into ballet school. She couldn't understand what was making him so grumpy. He hadn't even bothered to congratulate her properly. She'd been careful to tell him the news before any of the others, and all he'd said was, "Oh, that's good."

"I thought you'd be *pleased* for me," she had said.

"I am pleased for you."

"Then why are you being so horrible?"

This time he didn't deny that he was being horrible. Keeping his eyes fixed firmly on the ground, he muttered, "Thought we were going to go into ninth-grade Science together in September."

Nicola, too, had thought they would be going into it together. She had never seriously dreamed that Mrs. French would suggest she try for ballet school. She had never seriously dreamed that having tried for it, she would actually be offered a place. Even now she had to shake herself in order to believe it. The fact that this time next September Denny would be in ninth-grade Science all by himself and she would be at Kendra Hall still hadn't properly sunk in.

"Won't be the same," said Denny.

"No—" For the first time she realized it. Everything from now on was going to be quite different.

Rose always said that that was what was so wonderful about being in the theater. "It's all so *different*. You never have time to get bored. I'd rather *die* than have to be in the same place seeing the same people every day."

Nicola wasn't like Rose. She preferred a certain sameness in her life. She actually liked seeing familiar faces all around her and having the comfort of a set routine. Rose, at the age of eleven, had left elementary school and gone off to stage school at Ida Johnson without so much as a backward glance. When Nicola, a year before that, had moved up from elementary to Streatham, she had not only gone around to every single member of the staff begging for autographs but even kept all her old notebooks and report cards locked away in a big black metal box with the words CHAS FAULKENDER, DEC'D written on it in white lettering, which had been given to her by the

man who lived next door. Over CHAS FAULKENDER,
DEC'D she had stuck a label saying *Nicola
Bruce, 10 Fenning Road, Streatham, London, England,
Great Britain, The World, Private Papers, NOT TO BE
OPENED UNTIL THE YEAR 2,000*. Rose said she was com-
pletely raving mad.

"Won't be able to walk over to the park no more,"
said Denny.

"We could if I got home early enough."

"All the way from London?"

No, she supposed not. Rose only had to come from
South Kensington; Ealing was miles farther away.

"We'll still be able to go to soccer games," she said.

"Yeah, but it won't be the same."

When Nicola arrived home, there were two letters
waiting by the side of her plate. This time Mrs. Bruce
had not opened them.

"One's from Auntie Becky," she said. "I don't know
who the other's from. It's local."

Auntie Becky had sent a card with a scene from
Coppélia on the front of it. Inside it said, *Congratula-
tions! All our love, Auntie Becky, Uncle Andrew,
Lorna, Doug, and Lucy. XXX*.

"Isn't that nice?" said Mrs. Bruce. "All the way
from Scotland. Gran-up-north must have phoned
them."

In the other envelope was a card with a funny picture of a mouse drinking from a glass of champagne.
Nicola couldn't think who had sent it until she looked
inside and saw, *Good old Supermouse! I always knew
you could do it. Love and kisses from your friendly
neighborhood photographer.*

Her mother said, "Oh, that must be Mr. French!"

"It's not Mr. French," said Nicola. "It's Mr. Marlowe."

"Mr. Marlowe? Who's Mr. Marlowe?"

Didn't her mother remember *anything?"*

"He's the one who produced the mime show—that time they wanted me instead of Rose."

Her mother glanced nervously toward the kitchen door. Nicola guessed that Rose must be somewhere out there.

"Why should he be sending you a card?"

Why shouldn't he? She and Mr. Marlowe had been friends.

"He used to call me Supermouse."

"So what's this bit about your friendly neighborhood photographer?"

"That's a joke," said Nicola. " 'Cause he played a photographer in the mime show."

"Hmm." Mrs. Bruce still seemed doubtful, as if secretly inside herself she was still convinced that it was Mr. French. She picked the cards up and put them on top of the kitchen cabinet. "You'll have to start a scrapbook. Remind me tomorrow. I'll go and buy you one. Incidentally"—she opened the refrigerator, pushing Ben's head out of the way as she did so, Ben's head having a tendency to get into refrigerators and help itself—"Mrs. Kemp asked me whether she could have your blazer for Alison, since you won't be going back to Streatham next term."

"What for?" She resented her blazer being given away, especially to someone like Alison Kemp, who had once gone screaming home to her mother complaining that "Nicola Bruce made her dog go after me." She hadn't made Ben go after her. You couldn't make Ben go after anyone, probably not even a burglar. He was far too sloppy. All he'd done was jump up to say hello and accidentally knocked her over. "What's she want my blazer for?"

"It would come in very handy," said Mrs. Bruce. "Assuming, of course, there's any wear left in it."

"I don't expect there will be." There jolly well *wouldn't* be, if she had anything to do with it. The thought of Alison Kemp inside her blazer made her feel quite sick.

"It shouldn't be in too bad a state," said Mrs. Bruce. "Especially if it's a hot summer and you don't wear it all that much."

She would wear it and wear it as hard as she could. She would wear it even if it gave her heat stroke— even if it sweated her nearly to *death*.

"Anyway, I told Mrs. Kemp she'd be welcome to it, so if you could just refrain from doing anything silly—"

What could she do that was silly?

"I could accidentally set fire to it," she said, "with a box of matches."

Mrs. Bruce placed the milk on the table and pushed Ben's paws back where they belonged, on the floor.

"Really, Nicola," she said, "I don't know why you're being such a crab about this. *You'll* be at Kendra Hall—*you* won't need the blazer anymore."

On Friday in biology class, Miss Richardson said they were going to dissect a mouse.

"It's a mouse that Toby brought in, so I thought we'd take the opportunity to open it up."

Toby was Miss Richardson's cat and quite often brought her presents of small creatures that he had slaughtered. Miss Richardson didn't believe in wantonly killing animals just so people could dissect them. She preferred to use slides and organs already pickled in formaldehyde. But as she said, you couldn't stop a cat from following the course of nature. It was sad when Toby killed baby birds and tiny little creeping things that did no one any harm, but once he had done so, it seemed silly not to make use of them.

Everyone gathered around to watch as Miss Richardson, in her white lab coat, neatly made the first incision. Sarah and Janice Martin both turned away. Sarah was genuinely squeamish, and Janice Martin liked to pretend to be so because she thought it showed how sensitive she was.

"Poor little thing," said Miss Richardson. "It was pregnant. Look."

Nicola craned forward to see. She would never have killed a mouse herself, any more than Miss Richardson would have. Nicola had once had a mouse of her own, a white one with brown ears called Humphrey. Rose had been terrified and yelled every time she saw him so that in the end Mrs. Bruce had set him loose in the garden, where almost certainly he would have fallen prey to a marauding monster like Toby. Nicola couldn't have watched Humphrey being dissected to save her life, but this was a mouse quite unknown to her.

"What's that?" She pointed. "Is that the liver?"

"That's right. Do you want to try taking it out?"

Nicola held out her hand eagerly for the dissecting

knife. Cheryl said, *"Ugh!"* Linda Baker made a vomiting noise.

"Just think," said Miss Richardson pleasantly, "this is what we all look like inside."

Someone said, "Imagine being a *surgeon* . . . having to cut people up."

Linda Baker retched again. Cheryl said, "I couldn't."

"I could," said Nicola. She thought it would be fascinating, poking around inside people's bodies, taking out those bits that weren't any good anymore, patching up other bits that had gotten broken or gone wrong. She wondered if she would rather be a surgeon that an ordinary doctor, just listening to heartbeats and handing out medicines. Surgery would probably be more exciting. Perhaps she might even perfect some marvelous technique for transplanting organs that had never been transplanted before, such as stomachs or windpipes or something. Stomach transplants sounded as if they might be possible. She looked down at the mouse, working out how it could be done.

"Can I take its stomach out as well?"

"Yes, all right," said Miss Richardson. "Unless there's anyone else who'd like to try?"

Silence. (Apart from another retch from Linda Baker and another shudder from Cheryl.)

"Go ahead, then," said Miss Richardson. "Be very careful."

It was strange, but when Nicola was given a needle and thread and told to sew a hem, she instantly became all thumbs. Her stitches, huge and all too visible, galloped wildly about in zigzag fashion, and almost always the material ended up splotched with blood, so that now Mrs. Hibbert insisted she choose only dark colors so the bloodstains wouldn't show. When it came to dissecting a mouse, which was a far more delicate task, since a mouse was so incredibly tiny, her fingers behaved themselves perfectly without any of their usual clumsiness.

"Excellent!" said Miss Richardson. "What a nice, neat job! You really seem to have a feel for it. Have you ever actually thought of becoming a surgeon, Nicola?"

There was a moment's pause. Nicola waited for some loudmouth, such as Linda Baker, to say, "She's going to be a dancer," but nobody did. They were probably all waiting for her to say it herself. Awkwardly she said, "I did think once that I might like to be a doctor."

"Well, try thinking about being a surgeon. We could do with a few more women in that field. It's still very much a male preserve." Miss Richardson nodded as she took back her dissecting knife. "Remind me to have a serious talk with you about it next fall, to discuss the possibilities. It might well be something you could work toward."

Again Nicola waited for someone to say, "She won't be here next fall." Again nobody did. The class continued, but somehow for Nicola the joy had gone out of it.

"Why didn't you *tell* her?" hissed Cheryl as they filed out at the end.

"I thought she'd know." In her terrible conceit, she had thought that everyone would know—everyone from Mr. Henry down to the lowliest and most insig-

nificant of sixth-graders. She blushed now to think of it. There were eight hundred pupils in the school. Who should know or care what one totally unimportant eighth-grader was doing?

"You should have told her," said Cheryl. "She thinks you're going to be a surgeon now."

"She'll wonder where you are when you don't come back next September," said Sarah.

"Why didn't you *say* something?"

"You should have said *something.*"

"Well, I didn't," snapped Nicola, "so you can just shut up!"

She raced off down the hall, bumping people with her book bag, heedless of the angry cries from the student monitor on hall duty, "No running! I said, *no running.* You there! Come back!"

Nicola wasn't as a rule disobedient—not unless there was a reason for it. Today there wasn't any reason—or none that she could see. All she knew was that for the second time in a week, she felt like crying, which was ridiculous. It simply made no sense.

She had gotten what she wanted. She had gotten a place at ballet school. So what on earth was there to cry about?

CHAPTER ❧ *Ten*

Every year in June Streatham had a Parents' Week when the school was kept open in the evenings for parents to come in and talk to teachers and look around the classrooms. In the past Mrs. Bruce had never bothered with Parents' Week. She had always said that she knew what progress Nicola was making from reading her report cards, so why should she need to come and talk to teachers?

"They'll tell us quickly enough if she's not behaving herself."

This year for the first time, she decided that it was her duty to attend. When Nicola asked her, "What for?" she said, "Because it's your last term there," which seemed a strange reason to Nicola. You would have thought, since it *was* her last term, that there would be less reason rather than more, but once Mrs. Bruce had made up her mind she stood firm. She was going, and that was that. Nicola was also going, and so was Mr. Bruce. Nicola said, "Why *me?* Why do I have to come?" Mr. Bruce, surprisingly, said, "Yes, all right, I'll come along. That's probably a good idea."

For her part Nicola thought it was a rotten, lousy idea. She wouldn't have minded if they had gone *last* June. In fact she would really have liked them to have gone last June. Denny's parents always went, and so did Cheryl's and Sarah's. Nicola had often wondered why it was that neither of her parents ever bothered, especially when she had done so well and had a prize essay pinned on the wall or had her name included in the Highly Commended List on the Sports Bulletin Board. They had never seen any of that, and now, when it was too late, they had to decide to go and to drag her along with them. What was the point, when she wasn't going to be there anymore?

"What about my class?" she said. "I'm supposed to be having a dance class tonight."

"I've spoken to Mrs. French. You don't need to worry about that. She says it won't hurt you to miss class just for once. In fact I think she was secretly quite glad. She's very near her time. She'll be having the baby in a week or two, and she could do with a bit of a break."

"How long does it take to have a baby?" said Nicola.

"What do you mean, how long does it take? It takes nine months! I thought you were the one that was supposed to be so hot on biology?"

"No, I mean, actually *having* it."

"Oh! Well, that depends. It could take an hour or so—or it could take all day and all night. When I had you, it happened so fast I hardly knew anything

about it. Rose, on the other hand, was an absolute little monster. Took forever."

It was good to know that for once it had been Rose
and not herself causing trouble, but that hadn't really
been why she had asked.

"How long do you have to stay in the hospital?"

"Not very long. A few days, perhaps."

"And then you can just carry on the same as normal?"

"More or less, yes."

"So how many lessons will Mrs. French be away
for?"

"Oh, I would think she'd probably give herself at
least two weeks, if not a month. But I'm sure she'll arrange for you to have classes with someone else."

"Oh." She hadn't thought of that. She had told
Denny that while Mrs. French was away, she
wouldn't be having classes and could go swimming
and play table tennis as much as he liked. "I don't
think I'd want to have classes with someone else."

"It's not a question of what you want, it's a question of what Mrs. French decides is best for you. Anyway it'll help you get accustomed to the idea. After
all, you won't be having Mrs. French when you're at
Kendra Hall. Where has that man gotten to?" Mrs.
Bruce looked in exasperation at her watch. "It's time
we were off. Why does he always have to go and dis-
appear at the last minute?"

"He went into the garden," said Nicola. "I'll get
him." She found Mr. Bruce tucked away between two
rows of beanstalks. "It's time to go," she said.

"Is it? All right. Tell your mother I'm coming."

Obediently she went back indoors and delivered the
message. Mrs. Bruce clicked her tongue crossly
against the roof of her mouth.

"Men!" she said.

There were times when Nicola really wondered why
her mother had ever gotten married. Nicola was sure
she never would, if she hated men as much as all that.
Luckily she didn't, so probably one day she would,
though just at the moment it was hard to envision it,
because how could you be sure you wouldn't quarrel
and fight? Even with Denny she had differences of
opinion that sometimes developed into full-scale ar-
guments, but perhaps you couldn't ever hope to meet
anyone you agreed with absolutely and totally all of
the time—not if you were the sort of person who
thought. Miss Richardson said it was very important
to be a person who thought.

Her father appeared, wiping earth off his hands
with his handkerchief (there was more angry tongue-
clicking from Mrs. Bruce), and they set off up the
road toward school.

"Where do you want to go first?" said Nicola.

"Well, I suppose we'd better go and see your homeroom teacher, shouldn't we? Miss Cameron, or whatever her name is."

"Camfield," said Nicola.

Mr. Bruce, who had been lingering in the main entrance hall studying the photographs of the school
soccer and hockey squads, called out, "Isn't she the
one who said you were an asset to the community?"

"Yes." Nicola cast an agonized glance over her
shoulder. Fortunately, no one was within hearing distance. It was nice that her father should have remem-

bered the comment, but she wished he wouldn't shout about it.

"Go on, then!" Mrs. Bruce gave her a little push. "Lead the way."

The classroom was empty apart from Linda Baker and her mother, who were talking to Miss Camfield, and a couple of parents. Nicola didn't recognize them, but they had presumably already done their talking because they were on their way out. Miss Camfield glanced up and smiled as she saw Nicola. She'll wonder why we've come, thought Nicola. After all, there wasn't any *point* in coming, not now.

"What's all this stuff on the walls?" Mr. Bruce wanted to know.

"Just bits of work that people have done that have gotten good marks."

"Do you have anything up there?"

"Bit of biology."

"Well, let's see it then!"

She led them across to her drawing of the inside of a rabbit, with all the organs done in different colors and neatly labeled. At the bottom Miss Richardson had written *Excellent work!* Mr. and Mrs. Bruce stood looking at it. After a bit Mr. Bruce said, "So that's what you do in biology, is it?"

"Not all the time. Sometimes we do plants."

"I think I'd rather have had a plant," said Mrs. Bruce. "I don't think the inside of a rabbit is very nice."

Nicola wondered what was wrong with the inside of a rabbit, especially when it was so tastefully colored and labeled. Perhaps it was the fact that it was a male rabbit. Mrs. Bruce thought all male things were ugly.

Once when they'd all gone on holiday with Auntie Becky and Uncle Andrew and their family, and Doug had been only three, Mrs. Bruce had complained afterwards that she thought it "disgusting that they let him run around in the nude like that." Rose had agreed. "Boys are so *horrible.*" Maybe if it had been a drawing of the inside of a female rabbit, Mrs. Bruce would have liked it better.

Other parents had come into the room by now. There was quite a crowd of them. Linda Baker and her mother left, and now it was Mr. and Mrs. Bruce's turn.

"We've never come before," said Mrs. Bruce, "but since Nicola's going to be leaving—"

"She's got a place at ballet school, I hear?"

"Kendra Hall." Mrs. Bruce nodded proudly. "It's one of the best."

"Yes, indeed! So everyone assures me."

"If not," said Mrs. Bruce, *"the* best—well, apart from the Royal Ballet School, I suppose. Not that I would say the Royal Ballet School is any *better,* just better known. Kendra Hall has produced some of the world's leading dancers."

Mrs. Bruce proceeded to rattle off a string of names. Nicola could see that most of them didn't mean anything to Miss Camfield. She wished her mother wouldn't do that. Miss Camfield wasn't a ballet fan. She'd probably only heard of Nijinsky.

"... and then, of course, there's Pamela French, who is Nicola's teacher. She *was* going to teach my other daughter, Rosemary, but Rose decided she'd rather go to stage school instead. Rosemarie Vitullo, she calls herself now. She's at the Ida Johnson School, doing very well. You may have seen her recently on television—the commercial for Dreamy Liquid." Miss Camfield looked blank. "The little girl with the mother," said Mrs. Bruce. "The one where the mother pours the dish-washing liquid into the bowl and all the bubbles float into the air and the little girl says, 'Mommy, I can see pictures!' "

This was frightful. The other people who had come into the room were starting to stare. Nicola heard Miss Camfield apologize for the fact that she hadn't seen the Dreamy Liquid commercial, and Mrs. Bruce suggested that in that case perhaps she may have seen *Children of the New Forest,* where Rose had played one of the children, or if not *Children of the New Forest,* then maybe *The March Girls,* where Rose had played Amy as a child, or if not *The March Girls*—

"Anyway," said Mr. Bruce, "about Nicola."

"We shall be very sorry to lose her," said Miss Camfield. "I shall be especially sorry, I don't mind telling you. I had her earmarked as a future hockey captain!"

Captain? Nicola stared and felt her cheeks go red.

"Still, I do realize," said Miss Camfield, "that ballet has to come first. I haven't taught Nicola for all this time without learning that!"

The conversation continued, but Nicola had ceased to listen. She kept thinking, *hockey captain* . . . Last year's hockey captain had been a girl called Karen Jacobs, who had won a scholarship to Oxford and now played hockey for the British Olympic team. She had had her photograph in all the local papers and had even been seen on television.

"Of course," Miss Camfield was saying, "I don't

think I'd have been allowed to have her as hockey captain because Mr. Henry would probably have wanted her for the Student Council, and then we'd have had a battle royal for her time, so perhaps it's just as well"—she turned to Nicola and smiled—"that she's going off to create chaos elsewhere. I just hope she comes back from time to time to let us know how she's getting on. I would be sorry to lose touch completely."

Nicola felt the backs of her eyes starting to grow all hot and prickly. She swallowed rather desperately at a cannonball lodged in her throat and couldn't bear to speak. (This was getting to be a regular occurrence. She was in danger of getting a permanent case of lockjaw.)

They left the classroom and went back down the stairs to the main corridor. Nicola had hoped that after Miss Camfield they would be able to leave, but Mrs. Bruce wanted to see the home economics wing "where you made all those incredible solid-rock rolls last year," and Mr. Bruce wanted to look at the science lab.

They went to the home economics wing first. In the kitchen there were cakes and pies and puddings on display, and in the needlework room there were wonderful examples of garments handmade by people like Cheryl.

"I don't imagine there's anything of yours *here*," said Mrs. Bruce.

They didn't stay for very long in the home economics wing. Mrs. Bruce insisted on speaking to Mrs. Hibbert, but there really wasn't very much to talk about. Mrs. Hibbert could hardly say that Nicola was going to be very much missed. What she did say (quite nicely, with a sparkle in her eye) was that "Nicola is without any doubt one of those pupils who will remain in the memory. I shall never see a zigzag without thinking of her hemlines!" Even that, in a way, was sad. She would have liked to do just *one* good hemline for Mrs. Hibbert. But she had never taken needlework seriously—that was the trouble. If she had planned to come back next year, she would have made a really determined effort and surprised everyone.

In the science lab, Miss Richardson had put the dissected mouse on exhibition. Nicola took her parents over to it and proudly explained how she had been responsible for removing the liver and stomach, but even though it had been a female mouse and pregnant in addition, Mrs. Bruce still didn't seem to find it particularly nice. She just wrinkled her nose and said that it "smelled peculiar."

There was a large group of people gathered around the front bench, watching as Miss Richardson demonstrated something.

"She'll be hours," said Mrs. Bruce. "There's no point in waiting here."

Mr. Bruce looked unhappy, as if he would have liked to wait and talk to Miss Richardson. Nicola, on the whole, was relieved. They turned to go, but just as they were on their way through the door, Miss Richardson herself came hurrying after them.

"Mr. and Mrs. Bruce?"

They stopped.

"We didn't want to disturb you," said Mrs. Bruce. "We could see that you were busy."

"No, no, that's quite all right! I'd finished. I was just indulging in a bit of idle chatter." Miss Richardson held out a hand. "We haven't met before, have we? I'm Jean Richardson, Nicola's biology teacher. I was hoping you might come. I've been wanting to talk to you for a long time. You'll probably have gathered from her report cards that Nicola's one of my best pupils? I don't know whether she's told you, but I have very high hopes for Nicola. Has she shown you the mouse we dissected?"

Mrs. Bruce said, "Yes, she has, but—"

"I told her she'd make a good surgeon. In fact, I thought perhaps next term we might seriously discuss the possibility of a career in medicine. I don't know how you would feel about that, but—"

"Miss Richardson, I think we should tell you"— Mrs. Bruce said it loudly and firmly—"Nicola won't be here next term. She's going to ballet school."

There was a pause. Miss Richardson turned a puzzled glance at Nicola.

"Oh?"

"She heard just two weeks ago that she'd passed the audition. It's for Kendra Hall."

The way Mrs. Bruce said "Kendra Hall," she make it sound like Buckingham Palace. It couldn't mean more to her mother, thought Nicola, if she *were* going to Buckingham Palace. *Nicola's going to Buckingham Palace to dine with the Queen. It's one of the best palaces there is. It's turned out some of the country's leading royalty. Elizabeth II, Prince Charles, Princess Anne, Prince Andrew, Prince something-or-other— what was the name of the other one? There were four of them. Charles, Anne, Andrew—surely there were*

four? Nicola wasn't very well up on royalty. She knew
more about ballet dancers and soccer players. But she
was quite sure there were four. *Robert? William?
Kevin? King Kevin. King Kong. King—*

"Get a move on!"

Her mother was pushing at her, urging her
forward. Nicola looked up, guiltily, expecting to find
Miss Richardson's puzzled gaze still upon her, but
Miss Richardson had already returned to the little
knot of people gathered around the front bench.

They left the school in silence. Not until they were
out in the street did Mr. Bruce say, "She seemed
really upset, that Miss Richardson. Really disappointed."

"Nicola should have told her."

"She really seemed concerned that Nicola wasn't
going to stay on."

"Well, she would, wouldn't she?" Mrs. Bruce spoke
impatiently. "It's her job. The more that stay on, the
better."

"Even so . . . you don't think we ought to recon-
sider?"

"At this stage? When she's passed the audition and
been offered a place?" Her mother's tone, quite
clearly, implied that Mr. Bruce must be mad. "We've
already written to accept. It's all arranged. It's far
too late to start changing things now. In any case,
what on earth would Mrs. French have to say? After
all the hard work she's put in, all those years of teaching her! You know she doesn't normally take pupils of
Nicola's age. She's sweated blood to get her into that
school! And you want to turn around and throw it all
back in her face?"

"I'm only thinking of Nicola's future," said Mr. Bruce.

"We're all thinking of Nicola's future! Even if she did stay on at school, there's no guarantee she'd be smart enough to get into college."

"Miss Richardson seems to think she would."

"Well, Mrs. French seems to think she's got it in her to be a dancer—so do all the people at Kendra Hall!"

What about *me?* thought Nicola. Didn't anyone care what she thought?

"Correct me if I'm wrong," said Mr. Bruce, "but surely ballet dancing is a very short-lived career?"

"Not necessarily. Some people go on till they're forty."

"And what happens then?"

"Oh, well!" Mrs. Bruce hunched a shoulder. "By that time they're usually married with a family."

"And suppose they're not?"

"Well, if they're not, they're not. Then they do something else ... teaching, acting, whatever turns up. I do wish you would stop raising all these objections!" Nicola could see that her mother was beginning to grow angry. "If it were up to you, no one would ever attempt anything. We'd all just sit at home and be like cabbages. This is a fantastic opportunity that Nicola has. I just wish that I'd had it when I was her age. Anyway, I really don't see what it's got to do with you. You've never taken any interest in her career before. Why start now?"

Mr. Bruce said nothing to this, and Nicola knew that as usual her mother had defeated him. They walked the rest of the way home without speaking, which was something that quite often happened after family disagreements. When they got in, they found Rose eating chocolates and watching television.

"Turn that thing off!" said Mrs. Bruce.

"No," said Rose. "Why should I?"

"Too much television is bad for you. Turn it off!"

"*Why?* I'm waiting for my commercial."

The television stayed on. Mr. Bruce went through to the garden, to lose himself among his rows of beans. Mrs. Bruce, tight-lipped, went into the kitchen to put the kettle on.

"What's happened?" said Rose.

"They've had one of their quarrels."

"Oh, is that all?"

Rose, unimpressed, went back to the television. Mrs. Bruce came in with a tray and four cups. She said, "You can take one to your father if you wish."

Nicola went out to the rows of beans.

"Cup of tea," she said.

Mr. Bruce grunted.

"Beans are coming along," said Nicola.

"Not too bad."

"S'pose they'll be ready for eating pretty soon?"

"Give them a week or two."

"I like beans," said Nicola. "Peas are my favorite, but beans are my second. Then sprouts and broccoli. And potatoes. Why don't you grow potatoes?"

"No room for potatoes."

"Would you grow them if you had?"

"Might."

There was a pause.

"Would you have liked to be a gardener?" said Nicola.

"Not full-time." Mr. Bruce straightened up, putting a hand into the small of his back. "It's one of those things best kept as a hobby."

He sipped his tea. Nicola fiddled for a moment with one of the bean canes.

"Would you say dancing was one of those things best kept as a hobby?"

"No use asking me." Her father shook his head. "That's your mother's province, not mine. She's the one who makes those sorts of decisions."

On Friday in biology class, there not being any more offerings from Toby for them to dissect, they went back to spirogyra, which was what they had been doing the week before. Miss Richardson didn't look at Nicola or pay any special attention to her, and once, when she put up her hand to answer a question, Miss Richardson asked Michelle Brown instead, but at the end of class, when everyone else was filing out, she beckoned with a finger and said, "Nicola! A word with you."

With a sinking heart, Nicola went over.

"Why didn't you tell me," said Miss Richardson, "that you were going to ballet school?"

She looked down at her feet, at the horrible proper shoes that Mrs. Bruce made her wear.

"Don't know."

"It's not like you to be uncommunicative. I should have thought, if it were something you were pleased about—" Miss Richardson paused. "I take it you are pleased about it?"

Nicola nodded.

"So why on earth didn't you tell me? Did you think I'd be cross, or—"

Miss Richardson waited for Nicola to say something, but Nicola just stood there, looking down at her shoes. (Awful, clumping things.)

"I must confess, I was a bit disappointed," said Miss Richardson. "When I have a promising pupil, I naturally don't like to lose her. On the other hand, if it's what you really want—"

Again she paused. Again Nicola said nothing. Miss Richardson took off her white lab coat and hung it on one of the pegs by the side of the blackboard.

"You mustn't think I don't like ballet, because I do. I used to study it myself when I was young, though I was never as good as you are. I'm sure you must be very good indeed if you've gotten into Kendra Hall. As your mother says, it's one of the best. It's just that ballet is such a terribly chancy occupation. If you stayed on at school and went on working as well as you have been, you'd be virtually certain to get admitted to college, and once you'd gotten your degree, it wouldn't matter two straws if you happened to grow too tall or too big or develop weak ankles or knees, or any of the thousand and one other things that could affect your career as a dancer. It would all be so much more under your own control. Do you understand what I'm trying to say?"

For the second time Nicola nodded.

"I've spoken to Mr. Henry," said Miss Richardson, "and he agrees with me. Not that we're not very proud of you! Don't think that. It's a splendid achievement. We just wondered whether it might be possible for you to postpone the decision for another couple of years, stay on at school, and then decide. Would that be possible, do you think?"

"Don't know."

"Well, think about it," said Miss Richardson. "Go away and think it over and see how you feel. Will you do that?"

For the third time she nodded.

"Will you? said Miss Richardson.

"Yes."

"Promise?"

"I promise," said Nicola.

She said that she promised, but she really didn't see how it was a promise that she could keep, for what was there to think about? As her mother had said, it was too late at this stage to start changing things. And what of Mrs. French, who had worked so hard, had sweated blood to get her there? She couldn't let Mrs. French down. She had to go to Kendra Hall whether she wanted to or not.

CHAPTER ❧ *Eleven*

"Ghastly." Cheryl thumped with a fist on her desk. She did it so hard that her pens fell onto the floor. "Ghastly, *GHASTLY.*"

"What is?" said Sarah. "What's ghastly? What are you making all that noise about?"

"Next term." Cheryl spoke with loathing. "General Studies is going to have *Slimy Toad.*"

"That's nothing," said Sarah. "We're going to have Horrible Hampton in Languages. He's even worse."

"Nobody could be worse than Toad."

"Mr. Hampton is. He's horrible—he's sarcastic."

"Toad's *slimy*. I hate him. It's all very well for her." Cheryl jerked a thumb in Nicola's direction. "She won't *be* here."

"Wouldn't be having Toad even if she was. Science has Miss Richardson."

Nicola looked up quickly.

"Who told you that?"

"Nobody. It's on the bulletin board. Next year's

study-program teachers . . . Mr. Hampton, Miss Richardson, and Toad. Can I borrow your homework?"

"No."

"What?" said Sarah.

"You can't borrow my homework. I haven't done it."

"Haven't *done* it?" Sarah stopped what she was doing, which was frantically rifling through the contents of her book bag in a vain search for her biology notebook, and turned, accusingly, to stare. "It's due this morning!"

"So why haven't you done yours?"

"I forgot."

"Well, I didn't have time." With all these ballet classes, and Miss Caston's piano classes, and Denny wanting her to go swimming, and other people wanting her to go and sit for hours drinking milk shakes, she hardly had time for anything.

"But you *like* biology." Sarah sounded upset. "You *always* do your biology homework."

So today she hadn't. Too bad.

"Just have to copy someone else's, won't you?"

Slinging her book bag over her shoulder, Nicola clumped off down the corridor, slap-thud in her sensible shoes, toward the science department. She didn't normally clump, even though her shoes were so proper. It was just that today she had awakened in a clumping sort of mood. To begin with, she had looked at her hair in the bathroom mirror, and it had been all limp and lank and greasy, so that even tied back into a ponytail, it bore more resemblance to a bunch of seaweed than to hair. She had grumbled to her mother over breakfast, "It's ugly, long. It doesn't suit me. Why can't I go and have it all cut off?"

Mrs. Bruce had said exactly what Nicola had known she would say. "You can't have short hair if you're going to be a dancer. Long hair is one of the prices you have to pay."

Another of the prices you had to pay was being thrown out of the extra gym class. Extra gym was limited to ten specially selected pupils from each year, and Nicola had been one of those specially selected right from the start. Last year she had even represented the school. Now Miss Southgate (who had once been in the Olympics) had left her name off the training roll and instead put a big red note at the foot of the list: *Nicola! See me.*

"As there are only a few weeks of school to go," she had said when Nicola had done what the note had instructed her to do, "I thought you wouldn't mind if I asked you to give up your place. Miss Camfield tells me you're not going to be with us in September, so obviously we need to find a replacement. I thought if I could just try out one or two people in the meantime . . ."

She had looked hopefully at Nicola as she spoke. Nicola knew that what she was saying was to please do the honorable thing and go quietly, without making any fuss. What Miss Southgate dreaded was tears and tantrums. That was what they had had when Jenny Roberts had been dropped because of a weak back. Jenny Roberts had behaved like Rose. She had sulked for a week and had practically gone into a decline. But Nicola was made of sterner stuff than that.

"That's OK," she said. Make out you didn't care. Make out it wasn't important. "I probably shouldn't be doing it anyway, now that I'm going to ballet school."

Miss Southgate had latched on to this gratefully.

"Well, that's what I thought. After all, ballet and gymnastics are really quite different, aren't they? I wouldn't want you doing anything that would put your dancing at risk."

No, thought Nicola. She mustn't *ever* do anything that would put her dancing at risk. Anything else could be at risk, but not her dancing.

Sarah and Cheryl caught up with her at the entrance to the science lab.

"She'll be really mad," said Sarah. "That's two weeks running I haven't done my homework."

Nicola grunted and bumped open the door, using her book bag as a battering ram. Was it her fault that Sarah didn't do what she was supposed to do?

"I was relying on you. I thought you were bound to have done it."

"Well, I haven't."

"You could always copy mine," said Cheryl.

"What's the point of copying yours? It's all full of stupid spelling mistakes. I'd just as soon hand *nothing* in as copy yours." Sarah, quite obviously, was feeling hurt. "I thought *she* was *bound* to have done it."

"I s'pose now that she's going to ballet school, she thinks she doesn't need to bother."

Miss Richardson appeared, looking brisk and businesslike. She was evidently in one of her let's-get-down-to-work-immediately-and-not-waste-any-time moods.

"All right, Michelle, collect everyone's homework

for me, would you, please? I take it there's no one who hasn't done it?"

Silence.

"Good." Miss Richardson spoke pleasantly. "That makes a nice change."

Sarah, with an air of doom, put up a hand. Miss Richardson's expression altered from one of pleased surprise to one of annoyance.

"Not you *again*, Sarah?"

"I forgot."

"For a girl of your tender years, you have a quite extraordinarily weak memory! At this rate you'll be feeble-minded by the time you're my age. I'm not going to have you in Sciences next year, am I?" Sarah shook her head. "Thank heavens for that! A whole year of each other, and you and I would really start to fall out. Yes, Nicola?"

"I didn't do mine, either," said Nicola.

Miss Richardson raised both eyebrows into her hair.

"Why not?"

"Don't know." She humped a shoulder, embarrassed. She had never failed to do her biology homework before. "Didn't have time."

"Not having time," said Miss Richardson, "is simply another way of saying that you couldn't be bothered. The fact that you're leaving at the end of this term doesn't give you *carte blanche* for neglecting your school work, you know."

She hadn't neglected it. She had simply had too many other things clamoring for attention. Having other things to do was far more of an excuse than simply forgetting. Miss Richardson held out her hand for the pile of papers.

"I'd have thought better of you, Nicola. You disappoint me. You're the last person from whom I would have expected such a slapdash attitude."

"I could do it tonight," said Nicola.

"Well, if you can rouse sufficient enthusiasm. I wouldn't want to drag you away from your more stimulating pursuits." Miss Richardson took the homework papers from Michelle and slapped them down onto her desk. "Cheryl! Tell us about the nitrogen cycle."

Cheryl, looking panic-stricken, floundered to her feet.

"The ... ah ... nitrogen cycle. Yes. Umm ... well, it's, it's something that happens to plants and things, when they're planted. In the earth. It's when the nitrogen gets into them."

"Yes?"

"And then," said Cheryl, "then"—sudden inspiration—"it gets out of them again!"

"Really?" said Miss Richardson.

"Yes." Cheryl nodded vigorously. "First it gets in, and then it gets out, and that's why it's called a cycle."

Miss Richardson turned away in disgust.

"We did this only a week or so ago. You're obviously another one who's heading for premature senility. Is there anyone here who still happens to possess a memory in full working order?"

Nicola did, but Miss Richardson just ignored her when she put up a hand. She asked Linda Baker instead, and even when Linda Baker got half of it wrong, she still didn't turn to Nicola.

"I told you she'd be mad," said Sarah, at the end of class.

"Got her nose out of joint," said Cheryl.

"That's 'cause you're leaving, isn't it?"

"And 'cause you didn't tell her."

"*And* 'cause you didn't do that homework."

"She's *really* peeved," said Cheryl.

Nicola scowled and swung her book bag. After a few seconds, with a giggle, Sarah said, "I bet I know who else is peeved." Cheryl also giggled.

"Bet I do, too!"

"S'pose he'll have to find another girlfriend now."

"Y'know who likes him, don't you?"

"Who's that?"

"April Harris in the homeroom across the hall."

Sarah looked interested.

"Is she the one with her hair in all those little braids?"

"Yes, and she's got this thing about you-know-who. Christine Glover told me. They all live on the same block, and April Harris and Christine Glover—"

Gossip, gossip, thought Nicola crossly. She was *glad* she was leaving. She'd had just about enough of all this.

That evening, over at the park, she said to Denny, "Y'know that hairstyle where people put their hair into all little braids?"

"Yeah," said Denny.

"D'you like it?"

"It's all right."

"D'you like it?" She was about to say "D'you like it

better than just an ordinary ponytail," but then she remembered her hair in the bathroom mirror that morning, all ugly and lank. It would be even uglier and lanker by now. Anybody would prefer anything to that. "D'you like it on some people better than others?"

"Dunno. Never thought about it."

It was probably true. Denny wasn't really into fashions or hairstyles. Sometimes Nicola thought that he wouldn't notice if she were to turn up wearing a grass skirt with a plastic bucket on her head. She tried a different approach.

"Y'know that girl in geography class, April Harris?"

"Yeah."

"Does she live near you?"

"Yeah, same block. Her brother goes out with my sister."

There was a pause.

"What d'you want to know for?" said Denny.

"Just wondered."

They walked on for a bit.

"D'you think she's pretty?" said Nicola.

"Not specially."

"Tell me someone you do think is."

"Apart from you?"

She blushed.

"I'm not pretty."

"Anyway," said Denny, "I don't like girls that are. Always looking in the mirror and touching at themselves."

"Sarah doesn't."

"Sarah's fat."

"She's not fat! She's plump."

"Don't like girls that are plump."

"So what sorts of girls do you like?"

"Girls that are all thin and twiglike." Denny stopped. "Like you."

They looked at each other.

"Wish you weren't gonna be leaving," said Denny.

A familiar hot, prickly feeling came into Nicola's eyes.

"Not gonna be the same without you."

Nicola swallowed. Awkwardly, still holding one of her hands in his, Denny set his book bag on the ground.

"Can I kiss you?" he said.

If Rose were looking out the window of a passing bus, she would see them for sure. By the time Nicola got home, Mrs. Bruce would have heard all about it. *I saw Nicola and Denny Waters kissing each other over at the park.*

I don't care, thought Nicola. I don't care if she does.

She didn't care what Rose saw. She didn't care what Rose told. Once before, Denny had been about to kiss her, and she hadn't let him. Kisses led to other things, to things that were undesirable (Mrs. Bruce had said so). Today she didn't care if they did lead to things that were undesirable. Next year she wouldn't be walking over to the park with Denny. If she didn't let him kiss her now, he might never do it.

She had often wondered what it would feel like, being kissed by a boy—well, being kissed by Denny, really, because she had never had any other boyfriend. She had known that it would be more than the quick peck on the cheek bestowed by her father. She had just hoped it wouldn't be like the big, wet, slobbery jobs that old Auntie Kit used to press on them every Christmas. Rose and Nicola had always dreaded the moment when Mrs. Bruce would say, "Give your Auntie Kit a good-night kiss." One year Rose had run from the room and refused to do it, which meant that Nicola had had to suffer an even bigger and wetter and more slobbery kiss than usual; but then the next year Auntie Kit hadn't been there because she had died, so that looking back on it Nicola didn't feel quite so badly about having been the one to suffer. It would have been too hideous and ghastly if both she *and* Rose had run from the room.

Being kissed by Denny, much to her relief, wasn't anything like being kissed by Auntie Kit. For one thing Denny didn't seem to have had as much experience, because the first time around he missed her mouth entirely and they simply squashed noses, which probably would have looked very funny to anyone who was watching. (Such as Rose, through the window of a bus.) Auntie Kit had never missed and furthermore had had lips like a suction pump. The second time around proved more successful. Their mouths met and pressed against each other in a way that was really quite agreeable and not in the least bit wet or slobbery, though the nicest part of all was having Denny's arms around her and feeling him firm and solid, with none of those awkward knobby things, such as ribs and elbows, that you got with stick-type bodies like Nicola's. Could he *really* enjoy kissing someone who was all thin and pointy? Maybe Mrs. Waters was right when she said Nicola needed fattening up. After all, who wanted to cuddle with a stick?

Denny did, apparently. He didn't seem to mind about her elbows and her ribs. He went on cuddling her for so long that people looking out the windows of at least half a dozen buses must have seen them. Vaguely, from across the park, Nicola heard the clock on the St. Mary's Church tower chime the three quarters of an hour. Denny stirred slightly.

"You got a class tonight?"

"Yep."

"S'pose you really ought to be going."

"S'pose so."

They kissed again, as another half-dozen buses lumbered past.

"You'll be late," said Denny.

"Don't care if I am."

"What about your mom? Won't she be mad?"

"Prob'ly."

Across the park another clock chimed. Nicola, reluctantly, peeled her lips away from Denny's.

"S'pose I'll have to go now."

A few more minutes passed.

"S'pose I really should," said Nicola.

Denny bent to pick up his book bag, Nicola to pick up hers. Slowly their hands linked; they sauntered toward the fork where they had to part. At the fork they stopped.

"S'pose you'll have to," said Denny.

"S'pose I'd better."

A bus lurched past. A figure was hanging out of a front window, waving. It was Rose.

"D'you reckon she saw us?" said Denny.

Nicola tossed her head.

"Don't care if she did."

Rose was waiting for Nicola at the top of Fenning Road.

"*I* know what *you* were doing. You were kissing Denny Waters!"

"So what?" said Nicola.

"Don't know what you see in boys. *Stupid* creatures."

"Denny's not stupid! He's going to go to college."

"Anyone can go to college," said Rose. She was prone to making sweeping statements, especially ones that were obviously untrue. "Not everyone can be an actress."

"Not everyone wants to be an actress."

"*Or* a dancer. Lots more people get into college than get into Kendra Hall."

Nicola didn't bother pointing out that not everyone wanted to get into Kendra Hall. She contented herself with saying, "Anyway, you tell and I'll *murder* you."

Rose didn't have to tell. Mrs. Bruce already knew.

"You've been over to the park again! Mrs. Kemp said she just saw you there with that boy. Dennis, or whatever his name is. How many times do I have to tell you? I *will not have you going over there!* If you disobey me just one more time, there's going to be trouble. I mean it! I simply will not put up with this constant flouting of my authority. If you can't behave yourself properly, I shall simply stop you from seeing him. You're far too young to be going around with boys in any case. Now come on and wash your hands, and be quick about it. You've a class in forty minutes, and you're to go to a different address, so—"

"Why?" Nicola paused in the act of saying hello to

Ben. "Why do I have to go to a different address?"

"Because Mrs. French has gone into the hospital to have her baby. She phoned me this morning to say she's arranged for you to go to someone else for a week or two."

"I don't want to go to someone else! If I can't go to Mrs. French, I don't want to go to anyone."

Rose giggled.

"Listen to her! Be asking for star billing next."

Mrs. Bruce didn't seem to find it amusing.

"You'll go where you're told to go, my girl! It's not up to you to decide. It's up to me and Mrs. French."

"Why?" said Nicola.

Rose said, *"Why?!"* and gave a dramatic screech of laughter, one hand pressed to her mouth. Mrs. Bruce, in a fury, turned and slapped at Nicola with a hand towel.

"You do as you're told and stop answering back! I've had just about enough of you and your bad manners. Ever since you got into Kendra Hall, your behavior has been appalling. You've been rude, you've been arrogant, you've been thoroughly unpleasant. You're getting too big-headed—that's what your trouble is! When you've had even half the success your sister has, then you can start putting on airs. Until then, just remember, you've a long road to travel. You're not there yet, not by a long shot. Now go and wash those hands and get yourself ready—and don't let me hear any more from you!"

CHAPTER ✣ Twelve

Mrs. Bruce hadn't been able to remember who it was that was going to take Nicola for her classes while Mrs. French was away. She couldn't even remember whether it was a man or a woman.

"I'm not sure that she said. She was in a hurry to get off. You don't hang around, not with a first baby."

Why not? wondered Nicola. Were first babies different from second babies? Had she been different from Rose?

She had always been different from Rose. When Rose had been born, she had had a full head of thick, curly hair. Nicola had come into the world as bald as a coot. Rose had been plump and bouncing and smiled at everyone even in her baby carriage: Nicola had been thin and fractious and scowled at people. There were photographs of Nicola scowling, just as there were photographs of Rose doing her smiling. There were lots and lots of photographs of Rose—Rose in her stroller, in a pink, floppy sun bonnet; Rose, simpering, with a gap in her teeth; Rose in her first ballet dress, dropping a little curtsy; Rose on the beach; Rose on the lawn. Rows upon rows of nothing but Rose.

She *hated* Rose.

No, she didn't. That was a wicked, terrible thing to think, and anyway it wasn't true. She had hated Rose once, but that had been a long time ago, before she had started studying ballet with Mrs. French. Just because she was going to have to take ballet with someone else for a week or two didn't mean she had to start getting all full of hate again. After all, it was hardly Rose's fault if she was pretty and charming and knew where she was going, while Nicola was plain and moody and kept getting into all sorts of messes.

The class that she was going to with this unknown person was held in the same church hall where three years ago Mr. Marlowe had given her the part of the Bad Little Girl in his mime show, in preference to Rose (only Rose had made herself so ill with rage and sulking that the part had had to be given back to her again). Outside the hall was a board that said, *NORAH SCHOOL OF DANCING, Norah Andrewski, Ballet, Tap and Ballroom, All Ages, Beginners to Advanced.*

Nicola stood there a moment, looking at it. She felt a strong temptation to run away, but where could she run to? To Denny's perhaps. She could spend the evening in his kitchen, eating fish and french fries and fattening herself up; but still, in the end, she would have to go home and face the wrath of Mrs. Bruce.

With feet of lead she trod up the gravel path and pushed open the door. Inside was dim and smelled of must. She walked up the corridor toward the big hall at the end. The door was standing ajar, and she could hear music. Typical ballet-class music. Plinky-plonky, plinky-plonky, *plink*-plonk-plonk, *plink*-plonk-plonk. Any minute now and she would hear the clumping and thudding of blocked shoes and the shrill screech of voices.

She didn't hear either. Instead what she heard was just one voice, a male voice. It spoke from inside the hall, and it was neither shrill nor screeching.

"Hi, there!" it said. "Is that Supermouse?"

"Mr. *Marlowe!*"

He stood before her, laughing.

"Who did you think I was, Miss Andrewski?"

"I didn't know. They didn't tell me." She wished she could throw her arms around him and hug him. If she had been Rose, she would have done it. Being Nicola, she was too shy. "They just said to come here."

"And so, of course, you feared the worst?" Mr. Marlowe, who wasn't shy at all, held out both hands. "So . . . come and say hello to me. What a clever Supermouse! Kendra Hall, no less. You must be feeling very pleased with life."

"Yes." said Nicola.

"Yes? I should think you'd be dancing on air! As for me, I could hardly believe my luck when Mrs. French said she was entrusting me with the care of her prize pupil for three whole weeks. 'What.' I said. 'You're being irresponsible enough to go off and have babies.' "

"*Baby,*" said Nicola. She looked at him anxiously. "She's only having one."

"Ah, but is she?" Mr. Marlowe wagged a finger.

"Who's to say it might not turn out to be two?" He waggod his finger again. "Or three, or even four?"

"She'd have known," said Nicola.

"But would she though? How can you tell?"

"They can," said Nicola. A note of sudden doubt crept into her voice. "Can't they?"

"Well, perhaps they can. I'm sure you're right. Cheer up!" He pinched her cheek. "It's only for three weeks. Now, why don't you run along and change, and I'll try to find some suitable music. We don't really want plinky-plonky, do we? People who are clever enough to get into Kendra Hall deserve better than that."

If it hadn't been for worrying about Mrs. French having twins (or triplets, or even quads), Nicola would *really* have enjoyed her class with Mr. Marlowe. Even so, she enjoyed it considerably, but still she couldn't stop herself from worrying. she knew that it was silly, because even if Mrs. French did have only one baby, and even if she did go on teaching, she wouldn't be teaching Nicola for very much longer. Perhaps it wasn't really Mrs. French that she was worrying about but something quite different. Whatever it was, Mr. Marlowe obviously noticed.

"Right," he said at the end of forty minutes. "I think we'll call it a day. That was very nice. Now go and put your street clothes on and tell me what the problem is."

What she probably should have said was that there wasn't any problem. What she actually said was "You don't think Mrs. French is *really* having twins?"

Mr. Marlowe cocked an eyebrow.

"What difference would it make?"

"Well—" She fiddled for a moment with a loose button on her sweater. "She might give up teaching."

"She might, though I doubt it. But even if she did, you're going to be at Kendra Hall!"

Nicola looked down at her button. Another twist and it would come right off. She gave it another twist.

"You are happy about going there," said Mr. Marlowe, "aren't you?"

"Mmm."

"You don't *sound* very happy!"

"I am."

"But . . .?"

Nicola glanced up at him, puzzled.

"No buts?" said Mr. Marlowe.

She dropped her eyes again to her button.

"S'pose it would've been nice if I could have taken physics and chemistry."

"And can't you?"

"Not at ballet school. There isn't room for it."

"And you would like there to be?"

"Well, just in case," said Nicola.

"Just in case what?"

"I mean—" She fitted the button under her thumbnail, pressing it down with her middle finger. "I mean, if I decided *not* to be a dancer—I mean, s'pose I wasn't *good* enough to be a dancer, or s'pose I grew too tall or something—"

"Mmm?"

"Well, then, perhaps I might want to be a doctor or something. And I couldn't be. Not if I hadn't taken the right subjects."

"Hmm." Mr. Marlowe stood frowning, arms folded, as he gazed down at her. "Are you clever enough to be a doctor?"

"Might be. Don't know."

"What do your teachers say?"

"They think I might be."

"Do they, indeed?" Mr. Marlowe went on frowning but not in a way that signified displeasure. She didn't have the feeling that he was cross with her, only that he was thinking. "What do your parents say?"

"They don't say anything."

"You mean, you haven't discussed it with them?"

Slowly, keeping her eyes fixed on the button, Nicola shook her head.

"Why is that?"

"She'd be mad at me. After taking the audition and everything."

"Your mother? Yes, I remember your mother. I suppose she's pretty pleased about all this?"

"And Mrs. French."

"If you're worried about upsetting Mrs. French"—gently Mr. Marlowe removed the button from under Nicola's thumbnail—"then you shouldn't be. She would be far more upset to think you were being pushed into something you didn't really want to do."

"But she's sweated blood," said Nicola.

Mr. Marlowe laughed, though not in an unkindly manner.

"She's also sweated blood producing this baby, and between you and me, I would say that as of this moment it's the baby that's the most important thing in her life. And the most important thing in *your* life must be making your own decision as to what you want to do. Never mind Mrs. French, never mind your mother—it's your career that's at stake, not theirs. And I'm sure I don't need to tell you that ballet, almost more than anything else, is not something you should go into halfheartedly. If you're not one hundred percent positive that it's what you want to do—"

"It's not that I *don't* want to do it."

"Just that there might be something else you want to do more. You know what I think?" Nicola looked up. "I think," said Mr. Marlowe, "that it would be a good idea if you were to stay on at school and do your physics and your chemistry and postpone making any decision until you were at least sixteen."

"*Could* I?"

"Of course you could! Sixteen isn't any age at all. I'm forty-six, and I'm still postponing decisions. And why not? Keep things as fluid as possible—that's what I say. Now, listen"—Mr. Marlowe put an arm around Nicola's shoulders, turning her in the direction of the changing room—"it's Saturday tomorrow. Why don't you go along to see Mrs. French and tell her exactly how you feel? I'm quite sure you'll find her sympathetic, and I know she'd like to have a visit from you, to show off the new arrival—assuming, of course, that by then it's arrived! I'll be going to see her myself, around two o'clock, so if you drop by about two-thirty, that'll give me a chance to tell her you're coming. And in the meantime"—he ruffled her hair—"I wouldn't say anything to your mother until you've got things settled with Mrs. French. Know what I mean?"

Nicola knew exactly what he meant. If it was going to be bad telling Mrs. French, it was going to be a thousand times worse telling her mother.

She didn't have any class the following morning, even though it was Saturday. Mr. Marlowe had said he would willingly give her a lesson if she wanted, but in his opinion she could do with a bit of a break. How did she feel?

Nicola had thought about it and said that perhaps she felt she needed a bit of a break as well. She had been having ballet classes on Saturday mornings for three whole years. She could hardly imagine what it would be like to be able to get up late and eat as much breakfast as she wanted and maybe meet Denny and go to the Treat Shop.

Mrs. Bruce was cross when she heard the lesson was being skipped.

"If Mrs. French had thought you needed a break, she would have said so! She went to a great deal of trouble to arrange for you to have classes while she was away. The man has absolutely no right to go canceling them."

"He didn't exactly *cancel* it," said Nicola. "He just asked me if I thought a break would do me good, and I said yes."

"It's not up to you to say what would do you good! It's up to me and to Mrs. French."

Nicola remembered what Mr. Marlowe had said to her the previous evening.

"It's *my* career," she said.

"It's what?" Mrs. Bruce turned sharply to look at her. "Mrs. French is the one who's been responsible for your training. She's the one who decides whether you need a break or not. Who is this Mr. Marlowe, anyway?"

"I told you," said Nicola. "He's the one who produced the mime show."

"I know he's the one who produced the mime show! But what qualifications has he got?"

"He used to be with the Festival Ballet," said Nicola. "He studied in Russia with the Kirov, and now he works as a television producer and does ballet programs, and —"

Mrs. Bruce wasn't listening. She didn't really want to hear about Mr. Marlowe's qualifications; she wanted to go on being angry about Nicola missing a class.

"It's not as if you're some ordinary, run-of-the-mill

pupil. You're not doing it just for fun. You'd think the man would realise. It's essential you keep in practice! I've half a mind—" She broke off. "Where do you think you're going?"

"Going down to the Treat Shop."

"Who with?"

"Cheryl and Sarah." She didn't particularly like telling lies, but there were times when you just had to. In any case, Cheryl and Sarah almost certainly *would* be at the Treat Shop.

"Well, don't go stuffing yourself with potato chips and soda."

"They don't sell potato chips and soda." They sold chocolate milk shakes and great big scoops of ice cream filled with nuts, and today she was really going to eat her full share. Normally she let Cheryl and Sarah scrape her dish clean between them but not anymore. From now on she was going to eat exactly the same things and have exactly the same size helpings as everyone else. She didn't care if she *did* get as huge as a barrel.

When she told Denny about Mr. Marlowe and what he had suggested, Denny first of all said, "Great! Means we can be together after all!" Then he promptly went and ruined it by adding, "Would take a *man*, wouldn't it? Not as crazy as women." After they had argued for a bit about the relative craziness of the two sexes, and agreed in the end that perhaps they were equally crazy, only in different ways, Nicola said, "And what I'm going to do first of all before I do anything else is drink two chocolate milk shakes and eat a whole bowl of ice cream and not give any of it to anyone, and if I get huge as a barrel, I just *don't care.*"

Denny looked alarmed at this.

"I wouldn't want you to get fat," he said.

She turned to him, indignant.

"You were the one who said I was too skinny! You said I'd waste away to nothing. You said I needed fattening up!"

"That was my mom," said Denny, "not me. I like you just the way you are."

"Honestly," said Nicola. She didn't know whether to feel pleased or exasperated. Sometimes it seemed you just couldn't win.

"I told you," said Denny. "Last night."

They sat for most of the morning in the Treat Shop. People came and people went. Nicola drank her two chocolate milk shakes and ate one whole huge bowl of chocolate twirl ice cream with nuts (and felt rather sick as a result) and enjoyed herself watching the expressions on Cheryl and Sarah's faces as they sat opposite her and waited in vain for their usual share.

"What are you *doing?*" said Cheryl.

"She's eating the whole thing!" wailed Sarah.

"S'pose I can if I want." Nicola picked up her bowl and licked it clean.

"You'll get fat."

"You'll get ugly."

"You won't be able to *dance!*"

Under the table Denny and Nicola squeezed hands and kept their secret to themselves.

"You'd better not tell anyone," Denny had said. "Not until you've had it out with your mom."

At half past two, all filled up with ice cream and chocolate milk shake and feeling sicker than ever, Nicola arrived at the hospital. Denny had come with her, to help her find the ward and to give her some support.

"I won't actually come right *in*. I'll just wait by the door."

Nicola had never visited anyone in the hospital before. She would have been happier if Denny *had* actually come right in, but he wouldn't. He took one look at all the mothers and the babies and backed away, nervously, down the corridor.

"You've turned all pale," said Nicola, and she giggled because she was feeling rather that way herself.

"Shuddup!" Denny gave her a shove. "Just get in there and do it. Sooner you tell her, sooner we can get out."

The maternity ward was swarming with people. Just outside by the door, there was a large sign that said, ONLY TWO VISITORS TO A BED, PLEASE, but it looked to Nicola as though entire families had come, complete with picnic baskets and folding chairs as if they were on a day's outing. She couldn't see any doctors or nurses anywhere. Awkwardly, clutching the wilting bunch of flowers she had picked from the garden that morning, she walked on tiptoe down the ward hall. Suddenly, above the hubbub, she heard a voice, "Supermouse! Over here!"

She looked up, and there was Mrs. French, sitting in bed in a white, fluffy bed jacket with her hair all around her shoulders, with Mr. French sitting on one side of her, holding something that must presumably be the baby, and Mr. Marlowe on the other side, helping himself to grapes. He waved at her.

"Come on over. I'm just on my way."

"Having almost entirely demolished the bunch of grapes you were thoughtful enough to bring with you"—Mrs. French slapped at Mr. Marlowe's hand—"leave them alone! I'm the invalid, not you. Nicola, how sweet of you to come! Are those flowers for me? I'll get one of the nurses to find a vase. Colin! Show Nicola the baby. Isn't she something, Nicola? I'm told newborn babies are always like that—all red and angry and sort of *crumpled*. I suppose she'll grow out of it. We're calling her Anna, by the way, in the hope she may turn out to be a second Anna Pavlova, but that's probably only wishful thinking. She'll probably grow up to have two right feet and thump around like an elephant."

"Nonsense!" said Mr. Marlowe. "She'll be beautiful and sylphlike, just like her mother. Look at her! The spittin' image."

"Thank you so much," said Mrs. French.

"Don't mention it."

"And don't eat my grapes!"

Mr. French was holding out the baby for Nicola to see. She peered at it shyly. (She hoped she wasn't expected to *take* it?) Mrs. French was quite right. It *was* all red and crumpled. Nicola supposed it must be the result of having been scrunched up inside someone for nine months.

"Funny little feet," she said.

"Dancer's feet," said Mr. Marlowe.

"Elephant's feet," said Mrs. French.

"Whichever—" Mr. French gathered the baby back into his arms. Nicola wondered if Mr. Bruce had ever held her or Rose like that. It was very difficult to imagine. "Whether they're dancer's feet or elephant's feet, the one thing we would never do is push her into a dancing career against her will."

"Absolutely not!" Mrs. French looked across, quite seriously, at Nicola. "That's one thing you can be very certain of."

"So there you are," said Mr. Marlowe. "What did I tell you?" As he stood up to go, he winked at Nicola and pushed a grape into her mouth. "Keep things fluid. That's what I always say."

Nicola didn't stay very long after Mr. Marlowe had gone, partly because Denny was waiting outside for her and partly because she did not quite know what sort of conversation she was expected to make about newborn babies. She couldn't in truth say that they were beautiful, and perhaps it wouldn't be tactful to ask the sorts of questions she would really have liked to ask—such as how long it had taken and what it had felt like, whether it was like a cork coming out of a bottle or more like toothpaste being squeezed out of a tube. She might have asked if Mrs. French had been alone, but not with Mr. French sitting there.

"That was quick," said Denny as she reappeared. "You've only been gone ten minutes."

"That's all it needed."

"You did *tell* her?"

"Didn't have to. She'd already guessed." Then it suddenly came to her. "I think Mr. Marlowe had told her."

"So what'd she say?"

"Didn't really say anything, kept talking about the baby. But it's all right." Nicola slid her hand into

Denny's. "She wasn't mad."

"Not like your mom's gonna be. You just gotta tell her now."

They walked down the hospital corridor.

"Perhaps I ought to put off telling her," said Nicola.

They walked a bit farther.

"She's already angry enough."

"About what?"

"About me missing class, *and* going to the park last night. Perhaps I ought to put off telling her till tomorrow."

"Yeah, all right," said Denny. "Tell her tomorrow. That means we can go and play table tennis."

"All right," said Nicola. "I'll tell her tomorrow."

To get to the place where they played table tennis, they had to take a bus past the area of the park where yesterday evening they had been seen by Rose and Mrs. Kemp and then walk back down Fenning Road. As they reached number ten, Nicola hesitated.

"I s'pose really," she said, "I *ought* to tell her now."

She looked at Denny, awaiting guidance. Denny said nothing.

"S'pose I should," said Nicola.

"It's up to you," said Denny.

"I think perhaps I should."

"You mean, tell her now?"

"Get it over with."

"Rather than play table tennis?"

Nicola took a breath.

"I think it's probably best." She unlatched the front gate and pushed it open. "We can always play table tennis tomorrow," she said.

Jean Ure attended the Webber-Douglas Academy of Dramatic Arts in London. Many of the more than twenty novels she has written for adults and children have theatrical or ballet themes. She is the author of the widely praised *Supermouse*, an earlier book about the heroine of *The Most Important Thing, You Two*, and *See You Thursday* (an ALA Best Book for Young Adults). She and her husband, an actor, live in London.

Ellen Eagle graduated from the High School of Music and Art in New York City and the California College of Arts and Crafts. Her drawings and painting have won numerous prizes and the children's books she has illustrated, including *Supermouse* and *You Two* by Jean Ure, have consistently won her praise. She and her husband live in Glen Ridge, New Jersey.